ECHOES FROM THE MOUNTAIN

KAY CAGLE

Copyright © 2025 by Kay Cagle

All rights reserved.

No part of this book may be reproduced in any form or by any electronic or mechanical means, including information storage and retrieval systems, without written permission from the author, except for the use of brief quotations in a book review.

ACKNOWLEDGMENTS

I gratefully acknowledge appreciation to and for the individuals who have been contributors of their time and talent to make this publication possible. Special thanks to published authors: Betty Bolte for editing; Carla Swafford, technical formatting; K.E. Ireland, cover page design and Janette Spann for her support and advice.

CHAPTER 1

"Drive like hell. You'll get there."

Flickers of red and blue skimmed across the twisted metal bumper and illuminated the iridescent words on the tag. In the flashes of emergency lights, she saw the grotesque image of a mangled vehicle resting on its side in a water-filled ditch.

She sat very still in her vehicle. Everything had been all right when she pulled to the side of the highway, thankful for the darkness that hid her quivering fingers. The knuckles on both hands were set in hard fists from the death-like grip she had on the steering wheel.

Her gaze drifted through the windshield and lifted to make a silent plea. She took a deep breath and inhaled with her mouth open, needing all the air possible to fill her lungs. When it was released, a soft whistling sound filled the inside of the car. With one quick, determined jerk she grabbed the camera from the seat beside her and got out. Her steps were slow to accommodate the protesting leg muscles and spastic tingles shooting through each knee as she walked closer to the overturned vehicle.

It made no difference that the night air was cold. Beads of nervous sweat popped out on her forehead, and started to trickle into her eyebrows. All she needed was to take that last step, enough to make it across a long piece of wet carpet on the ground. She raised her right foot to clear the protruding lumps in the carpet. When the heel of her boot was secure, she shifted her weight forward to her right foot, clearing the obstruction.

A jolt of fear rendered her incapable of taking another step when a heavy hand clamped down on her shoulder. An involuntary squeal popped from her mouth. Her whole body bucked in protest. She was consumed with the cloud of horror that had plagued her life for almost two years.

"What are you doing?"

She started to respond to the deep voice, and its tone of cutting-edge authority, but her secure footing and weakened legs failed in the slippery grass, and she started to careen backward. A well-muscled arm encircled her waist and she was rock steady against a warm body. It was so unexpected she went rigid. If it had not been for the arm around her waist she would have plummeted to the ground.

"Who are you?" The sharpness of his words rasped harshly against her ear.

She struggled but the arms held her in an unrelenting vice. Fear stopped her breath. Her lungs ached. The silence of the moment screamed its desire to last forever. When the air in her lungs could no longer be held, there was a soft whoosh of release. Her body angled in a half turn and one side of her face pressed into a huge chest. When she lifted her head to answer, she stared into the dark, scowling face of a state trooper. The flickering emergency lights magnified darts of impatience in a set of narrowed eyes.

Her voice came out as a thin squeak. "I'm with the *North Fork Daily News*. Caron Kimble. I was sent to get pictures."

"That was a body you stepped over. You need to watch where you walk."

The bitter taste rising in her throat wanted out, but she swallowed and mentally begged it to stay and not empty onto the ground. That would be a total embarrassment as well as brand her a novice.

"Well, don't just stand there like a bump on a log. Take your pictures and get out of our way. We've got work to do."

The harsh tone in his directive pulled her back to reality and spurred her into action. He walked away, taking long purposeful strides, the beam from his flashlight making quick sweeps over the vehicle.

She aimed the digital Canon and snapped several photos, thankful for the emergency lights that gave her a visible point to frame the scene. *Lordy, why did I have to be working late tonight?*

A caller had reported the accident and she was the only one in the office. The night-shift manager buzzed her on the intercom. He wanted a photo and would hold a space on the front page.

This type of assignment was a first for her. It was not one she relished, but could not say no, being the newest employee in the editorial department. She was now living and working in a small town, writing for a newspaper where the publisher expected the staff to be diversified.

Her days of being employed with a big city newspaper had to be put on hold. The decision to move across the country to a small southern community meant survival. It was a good place to be inconspicuous. She needed a break from the dread that had stalked her for months. The unbiblical cord of fear had to be broken.

She paused to check the camera's internal memory to make sure she had photos and looked around for the officer, located him talking to a couple of first responders at the back of an ambulance. The other men got into the vehicle and left.

He saw her coming and started to move in the opposite direction. She picked up her speed. Being the new kid on the block, she was not going to let him get away before answering the necessary questions. Her manager was waiting and she had a deadline to meet.

"Excuse me. Is this the only vehicle involved?" She tried to keep her voice calm and professional.

"Dumb question," he said, the level of his voice so soft it was almost as if he were making the statement to himself. "You don't see any others, do you?"

"I was only asking in case one may have already been towed."

"One car. One fatality." The flashlight in his hand angled on her face, then made a quick flick to the camera satchel hanging by a strap from her shoulder. She was glad for the dark that hid a flush of heat she knew covered her cheeks as the beam of light slowed its pace and traveled over her hips and bare legs. She cleared her throat and asked another question.

"Do you know his name?" She ignored the rising stream of light as it returned to plant its bright focus on the book in her hand.

"Yes. But his family needs to be notified first."

"Can you tell me what happened?"

"No, not until I do more investigating. All I can tell you at this time is it was a single-car accident and one fatality. The driver was thrown from the car. He apparently died on impact."

"Did he have the seat belt on?"

"I won't speculate on that," he said.

"Can you add any other details? What is the make of the vehicle?"

She cringed at the brief snort when he aimed the flashlight back on the wrecked car.

"It's a '98 Nissan Altima."

"Not exactly a car for speed, is it?" she said.

"I didn't say anything about speed. If you notice the pavement is *still* wet from the earlier thunderstorm."

"Was speed a factor for the accident?"

"I don't know yet. It could have been a blown tire, and he might have lost control. The answers will be on the report tomorrow. This car needs to be inspected from front to rear. In the morning when I have more light, I'll come back and take a look for any skid marks. Ma'am, we've got to get this traffic moving. You've got all the information I can give you right now." He made a quick turn and started toward the mangled Nissan.

"What's your name? I need it since you're the investigating officer."

He paused and turned his head very slightly to look over his shoulder in her direction. "It's Bonner. Trooper Bill Bonner."

"Thank you, Trooper Bonner. I'm sure someone will follow up on the report in the morning."

"You don't finish a job you start?"

"I don't know who will get the assignment. I was working late and just happened to be the only one in the office when the call came in. I write feature stories."

"Well, then, we might see you around." He walked away, but his steps were a bit slower as he went in the opposite direction.

In the shadows, outside the circle of emergency lights, she groped around the inside of the camera case for her phone, found it, and dialed the office number.

"Daily News."

"This is Caron Kimble. I need to speak with Mr. Huston."

"He's expecting your call. Hold on."

She didn't recognize the voice of the person answering the phone, but there was still a lot to learn about personnel in other departments. It wasn't a long wait before he answered.

"Whatcha got, Caron?"

"A photo and enough information for a cut line—single car accident, one fatality. The officer won't release details until the family is notified."

"Bring it in. How soon can we get it?"

"I'm about fifteen minutes out and another fifteen minutes when I get in the office. I'll send everything to your desk."

"We're waiting."

Some of the body tension released when she got into the car. Her shoulders and upper torso sagged, but only for a second. The lavender fragrance from the air freshener suspended on the rearview mirror helped block the memory of a sweet, sickening odor that surrounded the wreckage. Her co-workers had talked about the seeping stench of death. She cringed at the thought it may have absorbed into her clothes.

Telephone poles started to become blurs on the way back to the office and she eased her foot off the accelerator. The deadline to complete the assignment would be met without a hitch. In her mind she had already written the information.

She was right on target as she parked the car and hurried into the building. Reaching her upstairs office, she paused in the doorway and leaned against the frame to catch her breath. The office lights were still on. She had left so fast she forgot to turn them off. The blinking screensaver on the computer monitor winked as she hurried to the desk. In an action as fluid as syrup flowing across hot pancakes, she extracted the memory card from the camera, inserted it into the computer slot, and plopped into her desk chair.

At first her fingers paused, then sped across the keyboard as she glanced at the information on her notepad. Words streamed across the monitor. She attached the photo from her memory card, clicked send, sat back in the swivel chair, and said out loud, "Done and done."

The tension holding her muscles prisoner began to recede, but she remained in the chair, pressing her feet against the floor. The gentle rocking motion moved the rollers on the chair. It eased backward. She extended her legs, slid down further into the cushion and propped an elbow on each armrest. Her interlocking fingers landed on her stomach. This did not satisfy her effort to relax. She stretched her arms upward and allowed her neck to rest against the top of the chair.

As her adrenalin level calmed, thoughts drifted to a cleansing, hot shower. She wanted to wash away the accident. Then she could crawl into a soft bed and close her eyes, forget about the tragedy of a human being who was a living, breathing individual one minute and nothing but a blob of dead flesh the next. She never understood how news journalists confronted and wrote about similar incidents day in and day out without suffering adverse long-term effects.

When she finally managed to draw enough energy to get out of the chair, for it had been a long day, she headed to Mr. Huston's office, wanting to make one last check to assure he had everything before she left the building. He was sitting at his desk looking at the computer when she took a step into the doorway.

She placed a hand on the doorframe and leaned forward. "Did you get everything? Wanted to check before I left."

"It's just fine. Good job," he said.

"Thanks." That's all she could say. After all, she was glad

to help, but taking pictures of fatal accidents was not her job preference.

Her shoulders hunched against the October night chill when she left the building. It was time to get some of her heavier clothing out of the storage bags, although she didn't have a lot of apparel to qualify for cold temperatures. That called for a shopping trip after she put a little more into savings. After the costs to resettle, she was beginning to see a little financial comfort.

A well-lit sidewalk guided her to the side of the building and parking lot. While the lights on the utility poles helped visibility, the outside perimeter of the parking lot was a forbidding sheet of ink-black darkness. Caron pressed the key to unlock the vehicle as she hurried across the pavement, her steps a rhythm of muffled thuds.

Her pace slowed when the skin on the back of her neck prickled and hairs stood on end. *No. Please. No.* Any hesitancy in her walk was stymied as she grabbed the door handle, jerked it open, and flopped down in the seat. She locked the doors and put the key in the ignition. Trembling fingers fumbled and pulled the headlight lever to emit a high beam.

Her eyes darted from left to right, wanting every shadowed nook and cranny on the side of the building revealed. She backed up and angled her car toward the street, having one thought in mind, and that was to get to the apartment and behind locked doors. As she moved forward to pull onto the street, her foot slammed down on the brake pedal. She gripped the steering wheel with both hands, feeling the pain of hard plastic digging into flesh. *Stop it. Just stop it. Take a deep breath.*

She sat very still, inhaled and exhaled. Breaths, at first ragged exaggerations, changed to slow and more even. There was no reason for her to feel panic. There was three thousand miles between her and the harassing phone calls, having to look over her shoulder every time she went outside. There was no danger. It was silly for her to even consider the thought. She eased the car onto the street and headed to the apartment without noticing the car parked against the curb about a half block from the newspaper building.

* * *

SWEAT SEEPED from pores on each side of Dexter's nose. It tickled a path to the corners of his mouth. A grunt of agitation filled the inside of the rental car. Heat radiated from his body so strong the front windshield fogged on the inside. One hand remained in a white-knuckled grip on the steering wheel. The other swiped perspiration ooze and dried it on his thigh. The arousal she caused grew. All it had taken was to watch her move. She had a way of sashaying her hips when she walked.

He had watched Caron from the rental car hidden in the dark shadows almost a block away as she hurried into the building. *I found you. You can run but you can't hide.*

His lips opened in a flash of satisfaction. Even he was impressed with his cunning abilities. It was easy to locate the newspaper office. A little visit to her friend's apartment in Los Angeles and he had discovered where she'd moved and worked—all the information he needed lay on the desk, an open invitation for him to look. There were even phone numbers for her apartment and workplace. It was fate. All he had to do was fly to Nashville, rent a vehicle, and drive the rest of the way.

When she disappeared from Los Angeles, at first he'd been angry. How dare she leave him. Then it dawned on him that she wanted to play a game, needed him to chase and find her to prove his love.

I know you love me. It was magic the first time we met. You made it appear to be an accident when you bumped against me at the deli. I knew the second I looked into your eyes you wanted me.

He had waited for Caron to come out of the building, get into her car, then pull out of the parking lot. He made sure there was enough distance between them before he turned the ignition key and followed. That night he would find out where she lived. If she wanted to play the game, he would abide by her wish.

CHAPTER 2

Bill allowed the pickup speed to slow when he got closer to the driveway. He shifted the gear lever from third to second. The turn was wide enough to accommodate the truck speed without manually changing to first. All he wanted to do was get inside the house and out of the regulation uniform and binding black patent shoes. It had been a long night and the paper work required when there was a fatality in an accident had to be precise and detailed. He'd walk back and check the mailbox after changing clothes.

The engine in his classic '57 Chevrolet Apache hummed like a mama singing to her new- born babe. He treated the truck like a pet. It had been his escape from reality on so many nights after he had it hauled from the junkyard and set it up on cement blocks in his garage. It took months for him to nurse the motor back to life and start the monumental task of sanding the body. It was the original rust bucket, plastered with pounds of sanded Bondo, but with the final coat of bright, fire-engine-red paint applied, he had stood back and grinned like a proud new papa. It was those long nights, willing his mind to focus attention on salvaging the truck, that kept him from going insane, drowning in memories of Katherine's death.

Every spare minute was devoted to the project. Working on the truck became an obsession. It took a year to restore the Chevy to its original beauty, and when the time came to close up the house, he stored the SUV, and opted to drive the pickup to North Fork from Mason Springs. It even had a name, "Truck." Truck had been his buddy, saved his life, and put him back on the path to realizing he had to start over. It just had to be in a different part of the country where his tormented mind could find some peace.

He was originally from New Orleans. After finishing a couple of tours in Afghanistan, his brother, the sheriff in Mason Springs, offered him a job as deputy. On the way to West Virginia, traveling through North Alabama he had fallen in love with the countryside, its mountains, the Tennessee River, and sparkling lakes. He promised himself if the job in Mason Springs didn't work out he'd return to the area. However, he had met Katherine. She turned his world upside-down and they were married.

He goosed the accelerator a tad to cover the distance from the main road to the house, anxious to get into his jeans. Before the truck stopped, he was pulling off the jacket. His hands were eager to loosen the tie knot and top button on the short-sleeved shirt. It would not be much longer before the weather forced him to go to longer sleeves. Token waited on the porch. Her tail wagged so hard if anything got in its path it would have been knocked for a loop. One leap and a bound got her to the side of the truck and she reared on her back legs, pawing at the air, then settled down and waited for the first head pat.

"My girl," he said, and squatted enough so she could push her head against his chest and receive the touch from fingers that dipped into her soft fur and massaged the excited muscles.

"Yeah, I missed you, too." She backed up and waited. "Okay. I know. We'll play, but I've got to get out of these clothes first. Come on, pretty girl," he said, and she trotted beside him inside the house.

It was a routine when he came home for them to check out the cattle. When the weather turned cold he'd climb aboard the ATV and she would lope alongside. Sometimes she would climb into the extra seat and ride. Bill left the decision up to her.

Token stayed hot on his heels in a "hurry up" mode as he hung the jacket and pants on a clothes rack, and scooted his shoes in the corner. He slipped the wide, shiny, black leather belt and holstered gun on a peg at the back of the closet. The jeans and boots lay where he took them off the previous night, piled in a heap on the hardwood floor. He sat down on the edge of the bed, slid his long, muscled legs into the jeans so frazzled this wearing might be the one to break the few remaining threads across the knees. Most of the back pockets had long since worn away and all that was left of the cuffs were frayed strings. However, it was comfort he was after, not looks.

"I need to go back and check the mailbox. Come on, pretty girl, let's walk it. My legs need the stretch after riding around for eight hours." Before he finished the sentence, Token was at his side brushing against his knee. He leaned over enough to rub the top of her head.

He had found her one weekend when he walked into the barn to get the ATV. She was laying in a pile of straw in the back stall, licking her front paw. When he approached she rose and limped to the nearest corner, cowered into a round bundle of fur and tried to cover her head as if to protect her face. He knew in his heart she had been abused.

She wasn't much more than a puppy. He kept his voice at a soothing level. "Hey, girl. Who are you?" He dropped to his knees in front of her and continued to coo reassurances. Without knowing whether she would snap at him, he extended his hand and very gently touched her ear. He sat down closer to her. She flinched and he spoke again, keeping his voice calm and even.

"Are you hurt?" A quick scan down her slim frame told him she had been without food on a regular basis. He got up, found an empty bowl, and went outside to fill it with water. Keeping his movements slow, quiet, and deliberate, he placed the water in front of her.

She raised her head, first to look at him and then the water—moved toward it with stealthy fear, the smell pulling until the temptation could no longer be ignored. She lapped eagerly, pausing long enough to look up at him with big, appreciative brown eyes before attacking the water in greedy haste. When she had her fill, she moaned softly and dropped back on her stomach.

"Would you let me see where you're hurt?" He kept his movements at a minimum. She whimpered when he stroked her leg with a forefinger.

"It's okay, girl. I'd never hurt you." His voice remained quiet and reassuring as he inspected the leg and paw to find the problem. A vicious-looking thorn was stuck between the little round pads.

"Oh, so that's the culprit." The dog whimpered again and rolled over onto its side to give him access to the paw. Bill, with one quick jerk, pulled out the thorn. She raised her head and licked his hand.

That had been the beginning of their friendship. He checked around, but no one claimed the Border Collie. She stayed on and became a part of the working farm, taking every step with him when they were out to check fencing and feed stations. He considered it a good sign and called her Token.

Token ran ahead of him down the drive and waited at the mailbox. Sometimes he thought she could read his mind. A flip through the contents of the box, and he pulled an envelope from the stack. He stared at handwriting he knew so well. It was a letter from Pat in Mason Springs.

As he tore into the letter, his footsteps took him to an old stump on the other side of the drive where he settled to read. He propped an elbow on each knee and leaned forward to focus every ounce of his energy on the letter. The other mail dropped to the ground beside the stump. Token lay on her stomach and stretched out her front paws.

Something dropped from inside the folded letter. He picked up a photograph of the most beautiful, little red-haired girl he had ever seen. He held the picture in one hand and began to read.

Dearest Bill,

We had some new pictures taken of Kat a couple of weeks ago and I know you'd want one.

She's growing like a weed and beginning the terrible twos age they talk about. It keeps me running after her constantly. She's so daring, and Allen says she takes after me. I'm probably getting a good dose of all the troubles I caused my mom. As they say, what goes round comes around.

How are you doing? Is the farm continuing to work in your favor?

I pray for you every day, and that you find happiness. We miss our friend.

Come visit when you can. Allen and I plan on accepting your invitation to come for a visit, maybe in the spring. We'll be sure to let you know. We are really looking forward to it.

Take care of yourself.
Love,
Pat

THE PHOTOGRAPH and letter were side by side, and even while he read Pat's words his eyes watered, riveting to the picture and the mass of dark red curls, green eyes peering out at him with such bright-eyed innocence. When she was born, Pat and Allen had written to ask his permission to name her Katherine, and nickname her Kat. It was to honor the memory of his wife. Kat was his nickname for Katherine. He was thrilled when he read the words, and could not halt the tears that streamed down his face nor could he smother the intense emotion, a mixture of joy and pain.

He carefully placed the photograph and letter back inside the envelope and placed it in his shirt pocket, then picked up the other mail and started back to the house. He laid the unopened envelopes on the side of the top step.

"Ready to go for a ride, girl? Just you and me, right, Token?" His answer was the fierce slapping of her tail against his legs. He reached down to scratch her ears.

Token knew where they were going and she ran ahead, jumped onto the seat of the

ATV and waited. Bill went on the opposite side to climb aboard and draped his arm around Token. "Oh, you want to ride, do you?" Before he could remove the arm she gave him a quick lap on the cheek. He chuckled and tweaked her on the nose.

There was just enough time before dusk to cruise around the west pasture where the Herefords were grouped for the evening near the troughs. They stirred at the noise of the ATV as it moved toward them over the hill, but accustomed to the sight, turned their attention back to the water. The feeders would need to be replenished in another day. The pasture grass still looked good but it would not be much longer before he'd have to start hauling out the hay.

Buying the hundred-acre farm had been a risk, but it had introduced a new joy into his life. Even though his knowledge of farming was sparse, residing in an agriculture county assured him of plenty of sources for advice, information, and suggestions. He was not afraid to ask questions. The farm was small enough for him to hold down a full-time job and manage a few cattle. It occupied his free time and that was what he needed. He had started with a couple of calves, then gradually increased the number to fifteen, and he was looking forward to adding to the tally. It would be his retirement haven and extra source of income.

He would not be sorry to say so long to the world of law enforcement. He had seen his share of death on the highways and often wondered why God would allow such tragic events to take good people...wonderful people like his Katherine. His views and opinions on many issues and beliefs turned raw when she was killed in a traffic accident, and he was on the cutting edge of disbelieving. He had to battle and control a cynical attitude that lay just below the surface.

People close to him kept saying give it time. But his answer to himself was, "I can't continue here without you, Kat." There was no magic potion to swallow and heal the pain of losing Katherine, and he did not even get to say goodbye. He had been left with a broken and contrite spirit and dreams that would never be fulfilled. Every day when he rose, grief met him at the door and he despised the world that kept moving as if to ignore her existence. He would no longer be able to hold her close or see her mischievous smile. Time allowed the pain to mellow, but scars, in the flick of a memory, would reopen and bleed fresh grief.

When he parked the ATV back inside the barn, Token followed him toward the house, the last glimpse of the sun's rays and the infusion of burnt sienna red, streaks of gold, and wisps of violet made him pause. What was it about the sunset on this particular evening? He had seen it many times and the fiery hues reminded him of Katherine's hair and how the sunlight danced and teased her kinky curls.

This sunset was different. He sat down on the top porch step, faced west and freed his mind of everything but the remaining colors in the sky. The image developed slowly, tentative at first like a child taking a cautious first step, and then it would not be denied.

The vision cleared. When he first saw her at the accident something stirred deep inside. She slipped. His arm instinctively reached to prevent the fall and when her body stabilized against his, a familiar sensation that had been suppressed so long began to smolder. It was as if he had no control over the beam of light as it floated over her body and allowed his eyes to roam with lazy curiosity. She had such a petite, slender neck and a small physical frame.

He knew she was staring back. It was so unexpected. It startled him and he backed up and became defensive, sharpened his voice to the edge of condescending.

That night he had dismissed the incident as being part of a bad day and dove into finishing the report. He would have to canvass the scene the next day. He forgot about her for the moment.

"Come on, girl. Let's go get supper." Token followed him into the house.

"A sunset is a sunset, isn't it, girl? What gives me the right to consider tonight's sunset any different. Just another figment of imagination."

Token eased her body against his knees and pressed.

"You trying to tell me something, girl?"

CHAPTER 3

Caron struggled to escape the persistent dregs of sleep and to be released from the nightmare. Shadows of fear played through her mind. She would suffocate if she did not get another breath. She lifted her arms to flail at the thing that blocked her path. The pillow against her face was the culprit.

It was the sharp pinging noise that finally drew her to a conscious state. She lay very still and tried to control a pounding heart, thankful to be in her own apartment. The metallic sounds were drops of rain falling on an abutting portion of the window air conditioner. She flopped on her side and pulled her knees to almost chest level. An involuntary shudder tweaked every muscle in her body when the picture of the covered lump on the ground replayed to her mind. She had stepped over it without realizing it was the body of the driver. She forced those thoughts into oblivion and opted for the uncontrollable sensations that had zoomed over her skin when she stumbled and was pressed against Trooper Bonner's body.

The pulsating throb in her throat slowed to a smoother

rhythm then regained momentum as she began to relive the reason she was forced to move from Los Angeles, why she had to leave a familiar life to get away from the terror that threatened her existence.

The events of that day were forever imprinted in her memory. She had placed her order at the deli next to the newspaper office where she worked, and whirled away from the counter to scout out a booth, but ended up in the arms of a man standing too close behind her. Apologizing for her clumsiness, she flashed a smile at him as she moved to the side and found a seat. When she looked up the man was gone. It had happened so fast. All she could remember was the man was about her height and he wore a baseball cap. A strange feeling had remained with her the rest of the day. The man had disappeared so fast, almost as if the collision never happened. She dismissed the incident as completely insignificant.

The phone was ringing as she'd opened the door to her apartment. She hurried to answer. "Hello."

"I love how you smiled at me today. I got your message." The voice was slow, the words distinctive.

Someone knew her and had a weird sense of humor. She had laughed. "Who is this?" When the unfamiliar voice initiated a stream of words to pledge forever love, she had held the receiver at arm's length and stared at it. She put the receiver against her ear again. "Who is this?"

Her answer was a click and dial tone.

The phone calls continued every evening after she got home from work. When she answered there was silence and a faint sound of breathing. She had shouted into the receiver, "You need to get a life," and slammed it against its plastic cradle. It was no longer funny. There were times she would not answer, but the ringing was insistent. At other times, she would leave the receiver off the hook.

On one occasion when she went into the office there was a rose on her desk with a note that said, "You are my life. Soon you will no longer have to hide your feelings." This was no longer some odious prank.

The episode that cemented her uneasiness was the night she and Bruce, her best friend and co-worker, returned to her apartment after having dinner. He walked her to the door and gave her a light hug.

"See you tomorrow," he said.

"You bet. Thanks for the evening."

She had just removed her makeup and was ready to get into the shower when the phone rang.

"Hello." The next words turned her blood ice cold.

"Who were you with tonight?"

"Who is this? Stop calling me. You're crazy."

"Don't take that tone with me. I won't put up with your going out with anyone," he had shouted. "Are you trying to make me jealous?" The raspy tone in his voice did not hide the anger.

"Who are you?" She found herself shouting back at the caller.

"The one who sends you roses and pretty words, sweetheart. The one you ignore every day. I'm right there under your nose."

"Where?"

"You'll find out when I want you to know, and until that time remember I won't share you with anyone. Do you understand? I better not see you with anyone else again. Is that clear? I'll be watching. Something might happen to your friend."

"You're sick. Don't call again." She slammed down the receiver, hands shaking. Her whole body trembled, at first in a revolt of anger, then a creeping paralysis of apprehension.

She began to make it a habit when she walked from her

apartment to the car, and even in and out of the newspaper building, to first scan her surroundings. More than once a warning chill crawled over her skin. She paused her nighttime excursions, and during the day, any man who paid her the slightest bit of attention became a suspect.

Stories about stalkers had infiltrated her thoughts. She understood the emotional stress that could drain a person's energy and clear thinking. To feel trapped, uncertain about what direction the danger was coming from, created a mental state of agitation day in and day out, twenty-four seven.

Living alone, she had developed independence, but this stress was too unbearable to handle, and she turned to share her fears with Bruce. The fear had reached a serious level. He had gathered her up, hustled her to his car, and complained all the way to police headquarters that she should have told him when it all started.

She related the incident at the deli to the investigator who took notes while she talked.

"I know it had to be that man at the deli. I apologized for bumping into him. I remember I was trying to be courteous and smiled. It has to be him. He mentioned the smile when I got the first phone call."

"Sometimes that's all it takes to touch a nerve with these weirdos. You never know what's going to turn them on. We need a description."

For the life of her, she could not remember much about the man's appearance. It happened so fast.

"He was wearing one of those baseball type caps but it was pulled so low I could barely see his eyes. I don't even remember their color." She paused and it came back to her. "I do remember the cap had some initials across the front. Uh…SUCS. It was sort of funny before all this started."

The officer informed her the description she gave would

fit several thousand men in the LA area. And since she didn't have a name, plus the fact there had not been any face-to-face advances, there wasn't much they could do. They could possibly track a caller ID number from her phone, however. "Bruce, that night we had dinner, he called after you left. He said I better not see you again. He said he'd hurt you."

"Sweetheart, don't worry about me. I can take care of myself. Our concern is you. Have you got dead-bolt locks on the door?"

"Yes, I had them installed when I moved into the apartment."

"You're welcome to stay at my place. I'll be with you at night. Then days, at the office, there's other people around."

"Thanks, Bruce. You're a real friend, but I can't let this nut control my life."

"Well, if you're sure. I'm as close as a phone call."

She had tried to laugh. "Don't mention phone calls, please."

It was the irate and belligerent call she got later that night, after Bruce had left the apartment, that frightened her so badly, the thought of leaving LA took seed. She knew it was him. Before she picked up the receiver, she grabbed a pencil and wrote down the displayed number.

"Hello."

"You're not listening to me. You were with him again. I think it's time I took him out of the picture."

"You leave my friend out of this."

"I have something of yours right here in my hands. It smells so good." She heard an intake of his breath.

"What are you talking about?"

"Have you been in your bedroom?"

She gripped the phone and walked to the bedroom. Her eyes immediately targeted the open dresser drawer where she kept her panties.

"Are you in the bedroom?"

"You're crazy." She wouldn't admit where she was standing. He had been in her apartment. How was it possible? Real panic set in.

A soft laugh threatened through the telephone line. "I can get to you or your friend any time I want."

"You broke into my apartment. I made a report on you at the police station today. I've got your telephone number. Now they're going to catch you."

"I think not. This number will only be traced to a public phone. You ignore me every day, so you won't know who I am until *I'm* ready. In *my* time and *my* way."

"Why don't you leave me alone?"

"In *my* time and *my* way, princess. Remember, *I* can get to you any time *I* want."

She hung up and called Bruce.

"I can't take it any more. I've got to get away," she said.

"Caron, you're letting him win. You've got so much going for you at the office. You can't give that up."

"Bruce, I need a break."

"First of all, I'm calling the police department. That jerk was in your apartment. They need to check it out. I'm coming over."

"You're the best friend I've ever had."

"Not so bad yourself, kiddo. See you in a bit."

Two policemen and Bruce arrived almost simultaneously. She watched through one of the glass panes in the front door. They stood at the edge of the curb and talked briefly. Bruce pulled something from his back pocket. She figured he was showing identification. Her door was open by the time they reached the cement stoop. She walked into Bruce's arms.

"Hey, kiddo. You okay?"

"Now I am."

Both officers had sidled around her and stood in the living room.

"Ma'am, I'm Sergeant Ivey and this is Officer Johnson. What happened here?"

She related what the caller said after Bruce left earlier as they all moved through the living room. "Here, Bruce. I wrote down the number. He told me it was a public phone and said it wouldn't mean anything."

The sergeant intercepted the piece of paper with the number. "We'll check that out." He slipped it under a clip on his note pad.

"Is the front door the only entrance?" the officer asked.

"I have two windows in the bedroom and a sliding glass door to the patio. There's a little gate at the back fence that leads to extra parking space. An air conditioner blocks one of the windows. Nothing looks out of place except the drawer in my dresser."

"And you said he got a pair of your panties."

"Yes." She could feel her face heating and she did not have to look in the mirror to confirm the red shade.

"Have you checked?"

"I have several pair, all the same color. I don't know. But the contents of the drawer have been tumbled. I keep everything folded and stacked."

Officer Johnson walked to the windows and checked the sills, then fingered the lock on the bottom sash. "Everything's secure here."

They continued into the dining area and kitchen leading to the patio door.

"Here's where he got in." The sergeant's hand was on the handle partially hidden behind the curtain. "The lock's broken. There's jimmy marks on the handle." He slid the door open enough to step outside. Officer Johnson followed. Bruce remained with her.

"I want you to spend the night at my apartment. We'll lock up here the best we can. I'll put a chair against the door handle for a brace. We'll get it repaired tomorrow," he said.

"That would be like he's chasing me out of my own apartment, and Bruce, if he follows me, he'll know where you live. He may already know, but if not, I don't want to take the chance."

"You got a choice. Either go home with me or I stay here, but I'm not leaving you alone."

"The sofa unfolds into a bed."

The officers stepped back inside. Sergeant Ivey said, "There's nothing on the patio. It's too dark to see any footprints in the grass. But that's probably where the intruder got in. And you have no idea who this man is?"

"Sergeant, Caron filed a complaint a couple of days ago on this man. He's stalking her," Bruce interjected.

"I know it has to be that man I bumped into at the deli. But it happened so fast I really didn't pay attention. I've racked my brain over and over. I can't remember his face. It was all a blur and then he was gone. The other officer wrote it all down in the report."

"I'll add this to the complaint you filed. Do you have some place where you can stay tonight? I'd do that if I were you just to be on the safe side," Sergeant Ivey said.

"I'm staying over," Bruce interjected.

"Good. Where can we reach you tomorrow if we need to get in touch after we follow up on this number?"

"I'll be at the *News Courier*. That's where I work," she said.

"Likewise," Bruce added.

After the officers left, Caron went to the recliner and plopped into its leather cushioning. Her nerves had reached the edge of the precipice and she was ready to leap into an abyss of oblivion. Adrenalin flowed through her veins like hot lava from an erupting volcano. She got up and removed the throw cushions from the sofa. Bruce was right by her side.

"Let me help."

"You do the unfolding. I'll get the bedcovers and a pillow."

Bruce leaned over and slipped his hands under the edge of the sofa and mashed the release. With a couple of tugs it unfolded into a bed.

When she returned with the bedding Bruce sat in the only easy chair she had in the room. He watched her as she spread the sheets and a blanket, fluffed a pillow, and tossed it to the end of the sofa.

"You don't have to go to all that trouble. I'd be fine just kicking off my shoes and stretching out."

The tears and frustration held at bay for so long would no longer be denied an outlet. When the faucet turned on there was no stopping the flow as two streams flooded down her cheeks and beaded on her chin. Bruce gathered her into his arms and pressed her head against his chest.

Between sniffs and hiccups, she said, "It's no trouble. I want you to be comfortable. You don't know what this means to me, having you stay, and knowing this maniac could be a threat to you, too."

"This is what friends are for. It would be his misfortune if he tries to pull anything with me. It would be my pleasure to see how well my fist fit against his face. Go put on your PJs and I'll tuck you in bed. We'll talk more in the morning. I want to do some thinking."

The phone did not ring again, but her sleep was interrupted by every sound in the apartment being perceived as a threat—the refrigerator motor, the air unit when it kicked on. Knowing Bruce was in the next room helped, but she gave up trying to sleep and rose about five o'clock and padded barefoot into the kitchen to make coffee. The first strong cup of black liquid helped her muddled thoughts become a bit clearer.

Bruce had slept on. His light snoring was periodically interrupted by a short snort before it resumed an even rhythm. Not wanting to wake him, she kept the kitchen lights dimmed. She sat at the dinette table and hooked a bare foot around each chair leg. A wisp of steam tickled her nose when her lips touched the ceramic cup to sip the coffee.

She could make out his form under the blanket, outlined by a soft beam of light that filtered through sheer drapes from the outside utility pole.

He most assuredly had the physical qualities that put him in a category of desirability, worked out at the gym on a regular basis. Women seemed to be naturally drawn to him. His bronze skin appeared even darker because of the collar length, ash-blonde hair, lightened by days on a sunny beach.

They had bonded on their first meeting in the break room at the newspaper office. She had just moved to Los Angeles from Seattle, Washington, and it was her first day at work. Pleasant introductions were followed by incessant talk as they discovered a lot of commonalities and especially a passion for classic movies, even the old black-and-whites. They became best friends with each having their own social lives. Bruce filled the role of the brother she never had.

He stirred on the sofa and she watched as he awoke and looked in her direction.

"Good morning," she said.

"Hey. How long you been up?"

"Long enough to have a full cup of coffee. I wore out the bed last night. Stay where you are. I'll bring your coffee."

"You'll get no argument from me."

When she had returned, he was sitting up on the side of the bed and had the blanket pulled across his lap. She had seen those muscular legs several times on their beach visits, but grinned at his sock-clad feet.

"I'll need to go to my apartment and get ready for work. I'll wait for you to dress. I want to follow you." He watched her. "I don't want to leave you alone until we get that door repaired."

"Thanks," she said, and left him to finish his coffee while she hustled to get ready. When she returned to the living room he was dressed, had the bed back in its regular position, and the covers neatly folded and stacked.

"Look at you. One of these days you're going to make some girl a fantastic husband."

A chuckle rumbled from his chest. "Yeah, one of these days."

When they stepped onto the small cement porch the sun was so bright she did not see the short, oblong box. Her first step kicked the container.

"What?"

Bruce made one stride and stood beside her. He picked it up and gave it a gentle shake. His eyes narrowed with the inspection.

"Want me to open it?" he said.

A foreboding chill started in her toes and made a stealthy climb. She folded her arms in a defensive gesture and nodded, then waited while he turned the box away from her vision and removed the top. His eyes and the expression on his face told her nothing.

He pulled out a small card and read.

"That bastard." His eyes moved from the card in his hand to the contents of the box.

"What does it say, Bruce?"

He held onto the card. At first she thought he wasn't going to let her have it. "Are you sure?" he said.

"I'm sure." The bold, black letters screamed a menacing

message. A cold vice tightened around her chest and moisture in her eyes blurred the words, but not before she read, "No one will have you." Her forefinger tilted the box for her to see the contents. She wished she had never seen the wilted, black rose.

"This man is a coward." Bruce raised his head and shouted into the air, "You're a coward. Come and fight like a man."

The only response was the yapping of a neighbor's dog in protest to the sudden early morning interruption. He put a protective arm around her waist.

Caron could feel her muscles pinch in an attempt to make her body smaller as if she were a target and attempting to hide, but her mind whirled with the decision.

If you're not mine, no one will have you. Those words were the catalyst for her decision to run.

CHAPTER 4

Caron pulled aside the drapes and took a peek out the window while the coffee brewed. Little puddles of water beads dotted her car. Well, so much for the meteorologist and his promise of a sunny day. Maybe the sun is sleeping in this morning. Her lips twitched slightly at the thought. It was a Monday and she needed to be at the livestock barn for the county steer show. The managing editor wanted a photo of the grand champion for the farm page.

This would be another learning experience since her knowledge of cattle was confined to magazines she had read since arriving in North Fork, but that was what the publisher meant when he said the staff had to be diversified. The move to Alabama was what Bruce had on his mind the night in Los Angeles when her apartment was invaded.

When she sat down at the dressing table the overhead light flashed through her bounty of uncombed hair. Chestnut-brown tresses, highlighted with streaks of champagne blonde, flirted with her shoulders as her head swayed in response to the pressure of the makeup sponge. It was cut in a bob, short on top and layered curls for easy care. She allowed a few sprigs to drape over her forehead. As she made the last vigorous brush swipes, she considered the image in the mirror. She had been told she did not look her thirty years.

The sun made a faint appearance through the top of the oaks on the opposite side of the street as she walked to her car.

Without warning her mind flashed back on the words written on that piece of paper. After Bruce had opened the container, all she could do was stare, first at the pitiful dead rose, then at him. Her eyes had scanned the other parking spaces near her front door as if the answer would be found out there, somewhere. She managed to regain control as the trembling subsided. Bruce had spoken first.

"Let's get to the office. I've been thinking about this. I have a suggestion."

"I'm ready for anything," she said and literally ran to get inside her vehicle and lock the doors.

They went straight to the break room when they got into the building. Bruce filled two cups with black brew and set them on the long table, just inches apart.

"Have a seat. Let's talk."

All she wanted at that point was to have someone else in control. She didn't feel capable anymore.

"Caron, I've got a friend. We were college buddies in the same fraternity. His father is publisher at the *North Fork Daily News* in Alabama. I can get you a job there no sweat, and you could get away from this monster."

She could not stop the exclamation in her voice and the squeaky tone of disbelief that came out of her mouth. "Alabama! That's so far from my friends and parents in Seattle. I've thought about going to stay with them. It's not right for me to have to interrupt my life because of some crazy person. It's not fair."

"I'm thinking of your safety. The police aren't able to do anything to protect you. You're my dear friend and I may not be able to keep you safe twenty-four/seven. Alabama wouldn't be forever, just long enough for this dude to get you out of his system. We'll talk with the publisher here, let him know what's happened, and get his support. What do you say?"

When all the problems had been analyzed and solutions considered, it had been the best decision to move. The deciding factor had been the police department calling to confirm the number that showed up on her phone display had been traced to a public phone at the bus station.

Bruce failed to mention his friend was the publisher of a newspaper in an agricultural county. At the time they'd discussed the change, she was in such an emotional turmoil she had failed to do the research.

She was so deep in thought she missed the turn to the livestock facility and had to backtrack. The grand champion was supposed to be chosen at nine. As she parked and glanced at the clock, she had only five minutes to make her way through a lot crowded with trailers and pickup trucks.

Now she was thankful for the last minute decision to put a camisole under the long-sleeve blouse, not knowing what the temperatures would be like inside the livestock barn. Her all-weather coat wasn't that thick. She had to purchase warmer clothing. Sliding out of the car, she put on the wide-brimmed hat that matched her coat and pulled it over her ears. A cold wind whipped at her bare legs.

The parking lot loomed before her like a treacherous gauntlet, smirking at her attempt to navigate over the gravel in open-toed shoes. She was still not acclimated on what to expect, especially in an agricultural county, and considered herself fortunate so far, not having carried her assignment back to the apartment on her shoes. It was another brief mental note to point this out to Bruce in one of the short letters she managed to write each week. She could see him reading and laughing his heinie off.

She sidled through narrow lanes between pickup trucks and gave a silent prayer of thanks on reaching the inside of the building. Small groups of men stood chatting, and she heard an amplified voice from deeper inside the facility. When she spied the extension employees, she shuffled the heavy camera bag to a more secure position and made a beeline to their table, especially to Barbara Graves, assistant county agent.

"Hey, Barbara. How much longer before they name the champion?"

Barbara had been one of the first persons she met upon arriving in North Fork. The extension office, satellite operation of a major agriculture college, was deeply involved in county farming events. With her guidance she was beginning to understand the difference between bulls, steers, beef cattle, Herefords, Black Angus, Brahmas, and chickens.

Poultry was a big industry in the county. Barbara had pointed out the difference, between guffaws of laughter, that putting chickens on and off jugs was a description of providing a continuous supply of drinking water while they were chicks. It was not putting the chicks in containers and taking them out when they were mature as Caron had mentally imagined. She made the mistake of asking and still got teased about her ridiculous summation.

"I hope soon," Barbara said. "I'm freezing to death, having to sit at this table. There's four more divisions and the overall judging for the champion and reserve champion. They're running behind."

This meant another hour. "I thought I was running late. Can you get away? Do they have a café here?"

"It's a coffee shop. Pretty good food and pastries."

"Let's go get a cup," Caron said.

"Yes, lordy. Anything to warm my hands. Just give me a minute to get someone to fill in for me."

"Hey, Caron."

She turned to see who called her name. It was Justin Woods, vice president of the local bank. He had a hand full of blue ribbons. Caron waved. He pointed to his head, mouthing the words, "like your hat."

"Thanks," she mouthed back to him.

"It's becoming," he called.

"Let you wear it sometime," she called, just loud enough for him to hear. Justin was another friend she had made only a week after arriving in North Fork, and a good one since he was vice president of the town's largest bank. She laughed to herself. He was wearing a custom-cut denim suit and chewing tobacco. He was giving out the blue ribbons. She watched as he hurried toward the center ring.

With Barbara at her side, they walked into the coffee shop and sat down at a small table.

Caron looked up to search for the slightly familiar voice that carried over subdued conversations. The tone did not have the same level of authority like it had exercised on the night she took pictures at the accident. It was warm, deep, and laughter resonated across the empty space to her table. She still recognized the voice. It was Trooper Bonner. He must have held her attention longer than she realized because the next sound she heard was Barbara's fingers snapping.

"Oh, Caron, are you still with me or are you on another planet?"

"Sorry, I... What was it you were saying?"

Barbara's wide smile lifted into a pleasant expression. Caron looked at her generous grin and glittering eyes that appeared to dance mischievously. "See something you like?"

"It's someone I met the other night when I had to cover that fatality south of town."

She turned her head and thought about speaking, or at least nodding in recognition. When her eyes met his, a jolt of heat traveled from toes to cheeks and she turned the color of a bright rose. There would be no denying the blooming inferno on her face. His gaze was steady and he moved slightly in his seat as if to change from an uncomfortable position. He turned his attention back to the man who sat across from him and continued their conversation.

"That's Bill Bonner. He owns a farm over on the east side of the county."

"He's the state trooper who investigated that fatality the other night. He scared me to death when he came up from behind and put his hand on my shoulder. I thought I would die of fright right then and there."

"Bill moved here about three years ago from Mason Springs, West Virginia, and bought the farm—has a few head of cattle on it and seems to be doing rather well."

"Well, he can sure be condescending."

"Bill? Ah, he's all right. He had a pretty rough time before he moved here."

"How so?"

"Well, I don't know the whole story, and I'm not gossiping, mind you, but I understand he lost his wife. They hadn't been married but a year when she was killed in a car accident. It took a real toll on him and he moved down here to get a fresh start."

She was looking in his direction, and it dawned on her he was returning her gaze. A fresh surge of heat made its way back into her cheeks, and the embarrassment multiplied to a new level before she could focus her attention back on Barbara.

"Are you going to be at the Farm City Banquet in November?"

"I hadn't thought about it. If I get the assignment I'll be there."

"It's not a bad meal for the chicken and mashed tater circuit. They'll be naming the Farm Family of the Year. It's quite an honor. Lots of farm and cattle producers attend, if you get my meaning."

She laughed. The humor of the thought created a slight jiggle in her chest. "Barbara, are you trying to play cupid? You're funny. I haven't been here long enough to even get settled. I've been too busy getting acquainted with the territory."

"Well, when good folks move into the county we do our best to keep 'em."

"You're the first friend I made when I got here, and I really appreciate everything you've taught me so far. Because of you I know a cow from a steer. But, Barb, I've got all the baggage I can carry and don't need to start hauling around someone else's problems."

"What do you mean, you got baggage?"

"It's a long story. I'll share it with you down the road."

"I've got to go. Darrell's back there in the doorway making 'come on' motions. They need me back at the table. Think about the Farm City Banquet even if you're not working it," she said, and pushed the chair back from the table. "Let's get together for lunch later this week. I want to hear about that baggage."

"We'll talk," Caron said, and lifted the still warm cup for another sip of coffee.

She kept her attention on the cup when she placed it back on the table, fumbled with her hands to straighten the napkin holder, then the salt and pepper shakers. Without any glimmer of doubt, she could feel eyes watching. She dared to lift her head and look at the source of her discomfort, thankful his attention was back on the man sitting across from him. He certainly had a claim on being handsome. Even the hunched shoulders and sprawling long legs couldn't hide the fact he had to be over six feet tall. A denim jacket stretched against his broad shoulders when he moved, and his hands dwarfed the ceramic coffee cup that rested on the table in front of him.

She continued her study since he was avidly engrossed in conversation and unaware of her scrutiny. It wasn't the warmth of the coffee cup she clutched with both hands that spread into her arms and caused chill bumps of delight, but a flashing reminder of her body against his when he prevented her fall at the car accident. A male essence oozed from the top of his head right down to every filled crease in faded jeans and badly scuffed boots. That and the fact she knew he was a state trooper added to the mixture of alpha manliness. And while the view was pleasant, she could look from afar and appreciate the scenery without having it affect her own life.

A couple of old, weathered hats had been tossed on the table in front of the men. The object of her attention ran long fingers through sandy brown, neatly clipped hair, then over a firm chin that had a day-old shadow. When she had caught his gaze on her earlier, she couldn't determine if that indention on his chin was a deep dimple or scar, but whatever it was it fit with the firm, square jaw.

The sudden movement of both men sliding out of the booth ended her study and she quickly settled her eyes back on her own table and cup. She was not prepared for what happened next, or the shadow that blocked the overhead lighting.

"Good morning."

Her head tilted back, and back, then back some more.

"Yes. Uh, it's Bill Bonner, isn't it?"

"And your name is Caron. I think they've finished the judging. Gotta go. Are you taking pictures?"

He turned to the man he had been sitting with in the booth. "Matt, I'll see you later this week on that calf."

"Sure thing, Bill," he said, and the man went in the opposite direction.

Caron grabbed her camera bag, and when she looked up he was standing and holding the thick glass door open. As she sailed through the opening, her movement stirred the air and she detected the essence of cedar and coffee.

"Maybe I'll see you around some time," he said, and turned to walk down a hall. That was the second time she had heard that statement from him, the other one at the accident.

She made a few steps toward the door leading into the auditorium and center ring, but took a brief look in the direction he had gone. He was still visible. She noticed his legs slightly bowed at the knees and his slow, sure-footed pace.

As she continued toward the auditorium, her thoughts fled back to one of the stolen peeks in his direction. It was the look in his eyes that remained with her. She had seen that look before, observing her own image in the mirror. The mouth was turned up in a smile and the lips were moving, but the eyes showed no emotion.

CHAPTER 5

When Caron saw the mounds of bagged sweet potatoes, doubt infiltrated her good intentions to be a volunteer for the church's Community Service Day. The pastor had made the announcement during morning service that individuals were needed for the project. Now, the decision was heaped with a pile of uncertainty. She parked her car and ventured closer to the hectic scene to at least inquire what the event was all about.

A swarm of activity hummed at the edge of the park. Youths formed an assembly line, unloading burlap bags from pickup trucks and stacking them on huge wooden pallets. She slowed her pace and looked for a familiar face from church. Unable to pinpoint anyone she knew, she was starting to consider her presence a mistake. She had no knowledge of what was taking place. A woman stood outside the workers, arms raised and hands gesturing directions and orders. She headed toward the voice.

"Hi, I'm Caron Kimble. Umm, Reverend Tom said volunteers were needed. I don't know anything about this, but here I am. How can I help?"

"Bless your heart. I'm Sherry Tubbs. We need all the help we can get."

"Uh, doing what?"

"These are culled sweet potatoes. They're hauled in and we salvage the good ones. Those go to charity institutions. The rest are moved to cutting tables where the bad spots are removed, then bagged, loaded on pickups and taken out to farms for livestock feed."

When the minister said, "Let your light shine" during the announcement this was not what Caron had in mind. "Oh, well, what can I do?"

"I could sure use you at the cutting table." A wide grin lifted her lips. "I don't trust these hyper teenagers with a knife. They could get careless and hurt themselves. That sure would put a damper on the project."

Caron was thinking she had wandered way out into left field, but had volunteered, so waded back in with both feet. She would see how deep she could go. This was her community now.

St. Luther's church wasn't the ten thousand member denomination she'd belonged to in LA, but on her first visit she felt a sense of warmth that drew her back for a second and even a third Sunday morning service. She was pretty much a regular, welcoming the peace, even though the possibility of returning to the big city was an everyday beckoning temptation. She discovered a sweet release. The stress of being pursued by the unknown had started to abate.

"Here," Sherry said, and handed Caron one of the longest, sharpest looking knives she'd ever seen. *No wonder they want an adult to handle this part of the project.*

Sherry picked one of the sweet potatoes and showed Caron how to cut away and dig out the bad spots. It was then tossed into a waiting bucket. When the bucket filled, the sweet potatoes went into a bag, tied and ready for its next stop on the delivery list.

It had turned unseasonably warm for an October afternoon. She removed her windbreaker and tied the sleeves in a knot around her waist, allowing the jacket to drape across her behind. She considered laying it on the ground close to the table, but watching Sherry cut away a rotten spot on the sweet potato and gunk fly when she slung it off the knife changed her mind. She did not want it to get splattered with potato goop. About five potatoes into the job, her hands and wrists were covered with a thick layer of rotten glob. She was thankful there was no odor.

The sticky mess was under her fingernails and her nose was itching to be scratched. She brought the inside of her elbow closer to her nose and rubbed it against her skin, relishing the sensation of relief. *Am I the only one who's going to do the cutting?* Her preference for sweet potato dishes would be put on hold for a while.

"You mean they let a newspaper woman handle a knife. Don't they know better?"

She jumped, hearing and recognizing the voice—then looked into the depths of warm brown eyes. They were the color of a fine Irish whiskey, partially hidden by tawny lashes. He removed his hat and brushed a hand over his head before replacing and pulling it a tad lower over his forehead. The slight detection of bold in the tilt of his lips made her respond. But she had to swallow first to get the saliva flowing in a dry mouth.

There was no running from the unexpected moment. She could not get around the buckets of potatoes without stumbling. Before she could get her senses back she was confronted with the fact there wasn't one inch of flab on his long arms and the T-shirt material let her know there was some real muscle under that shirt. Her view revealed the scar on his cheek. It was not a dimple or cleft she had considered when seeing him briefly at the livestock sale.

She shook the knife and allowed it to dangle in his direction. "You should never laugh at a woman holding a knife." Another playful waggle of the blade brought on a deep chuckle that vibrated his broad, smooth chest. The laugh extended to his mouth and jaw line, so firm it could have been sculpted and fired in a kiln.

"Would you care to join me? I'm sure Sherry can scare up another knife." Caron didn't complete the sentence before Sherry walked up and handed him a knife, handle first.

"Hey, Bill. You're just in time to help us get this job finished. The more help we have the sooner we all get to go home."

"Now there's a woman who knows how to handle a knife," he said, grabbing a potato and starting to cut.

His attention focused on the potatoes in front of him. She was too aware of the lengthy silence between them, standing so close at the table.

"How did they manage to hook you into such a messy job?" he finally said as he pitched a handful of rotten peelings into the bucket.

"They didn't hook me. I volunteered when they made the announcement at church this morning. They needed volunteers." She paused. "I really didn't know what I was getting into."

She noticed at the mention of the word "church," he kept his eyes cast down.

"Why are you here?" she asked, turning the table on his inquiry.

"Helping with the potatoes, and delivering them, wherever they need to go. They do this after sweet potatoes are harvested. Nothing's wasted. It all goes for a good cause. I've got a truck and the time."

"That's awfully nice of you, Trooper Bonner."

"Listen, as long as we're at the same table with equal sized knives, I think we can go on a first name basis. It's Bill." His attention remained on the potato. "I'm not familiar with the name Kimble. I haven't seen it on my rounds in the county. Where's home? I don't detect any accent in your voice?"

"I'm originally from Seattle, Washington." She hesitated. That's as far as she would go with personal information. "I needed a break from the big city life."

"How long have you been here?"

"Not long. Enough time to get my feet planted in the agricultural life of the community. Oh, goodness, I can't believe I just said that."

Another soft laugh lifted to a smile and he tilted his head for a sideways glance at her. "There's a big difference between small communities and city life. You don't get bored?"

"Actually, no. It's been a welcomed break."

"So, why did you choose a newspaper in the south? Isn't it a step down from the big city?"

The defensive wall started to rise, not from fear, but from needing a sense of privacy. He was getting a little too personal, but telling the truth prevented misunderstandings. He was in law enforcement, so questions probably came natural to him. "I have a friend who went to school with the son of the publisher."

"Nice to have friends to open doors." While he continued the conversation, he kept his eyes on the diminishing pile of potatoes.

With his help they were soon caught up, and several youths started to clean up the reddish tan globs of mushy residue on the ground. They wiped the sticky layers off the tables, and water was brought over to rinse the crud off their hands. Her fingernails would have to wait until she got home.

"Where're you going from here?" His question caught her off guard, but the calm in his voice made her answer with a light and positive response.

"Home. It will take me an hour to get taters from under my fingernails."

"Well, then, we'll see you around," he said as he took a couple of steps away, then his next forward movement seemed to lock his foot onto the ground. But he didn't look at her when he spoke. "Do you drink coffee?"

It was her turn to laugh. "Day and night, anytime it's brewed."

"Have you got time for a cup of coffee? Or a cold drink?" He waited for her response.

At first she considered refusing, but scrutinizing his expression and the fact that he'd removed his hat changed any opposition to the invitation.

"Thank you. That would be nice. Yes, I'll have coffee. Where?"

"Well, as soon as they get my truck loaded, which shouldn't take long, we'll stop by the North Fork Café. You know where it is?"

"Yes, I do." She laughed. "They have a great chili hotdog. I have lunch there often. I like the atmosphere. It reminds me of the old-time diner we have in Van Nuys outside of Los Angeles."

"I thought you were from Seattle."

"Oh. I worked in Los Angeles for a while." That answer seemed to be satisfactory.

"Do you want me to meet you there? They're not quite through loading, but it shouldn't be much longer."

"I'll go ahead. I'd like to get some real soap and water on these hands."

"Well then, we'll see you there," he said.

The North Fork Café had quickly become her favorite lunch hangout, and especially the chili hot dogs and cheese fries. Both were fattening and sinful as all get out, but she just had to eat lunch there a couple of times a week, ordered the same thing. The treat was so good that when she finished the last bite she'd run her forefinger around the paper containers that held the hot dog and get every bit of chili goody.

Being a Sunday afternoon there were plenty of empty spots in the parking lot. She pulled close to the door. By the time she went to the bathroom and washed her hands, Bill was pulling his truck alongside her car. And what a truck, a real bright-red classic. She didn't know exactly what it was, but sure had the curiosity to find out the make and model.

He opened the truck door and planted a steady, booted foot against the pavement, looked toward the café, paused, and swung his body out of the truck seat. She was amazed at the cat-like agility that oozed as his body moved. It was the determined expression that kept her eyes on his face and the taunting grin across his sensuous mouth. He glanced back at the truck and then at the café. When he came inside, he scanned the interior to locate her, and the set features on his face softened. She could see the slight tremble of a chuckle in his chest. He removed his hat. It dropped with a soft thud on the table as he slid into the booth.

"That is an awesome truck. What is it? How old is it?" she asked.

The waitress took their coffee order and hurried off.

His shoulders went erect with pride. She was aware of his pleasant sigh.

"I call it Truck. It's a '57 Chevrolet Apache sidestep."

"Now, that *really* is a truck. The motor?"

"A straight six engine with a three-speed manual transmission. The shift is what they call 'three on the tree.' That's a stick shift on the steering wheel instead of 'four on the floor,' uh, shifting from the floorboard."

"I know. It's a beauty. I have a friend where I worked in LA who was a real antique car buff. Sometimes I'd go with him to the car shows. Did you restore it or was it purchased as is?"

His face went solemn and for a brief second his eyes hazed.

"I found Truck in a junkyard. I wanted to restore it. Me and Truck spent a lot of nights together."

"Where's the ignition?" she asked, unable to suppress her own smile, "dash or floorboard?"

"You do know classics. It has the tendency to freak out folks when it doesn't crank until you mash the starter pedal on the floor, next to the gas pedal. It's an oldie and goodie."

"Those are the best kind. So, how long have you been a state trooper?"

"In this county, about three years." The fog in his eyes lifted and all of his attention came back to her.

"In this county? That says you've been in law enforcement in other places?"

"I spent some time as deputy in Mason Springs, West Virginia. My brother was sheriff there."

Barbara had related what she knew about the story, so Caron didn't pursue that part of the conversation.

He kept his eyes on her face. They remained even when the waitress brought two cups of coffee. She thought there was a question in there somewhere, but couldn't quite put her finger on the subject.

"Well, what do you think about your volunteer experience this afternoon?"

"It was interesting. When I arrived I thought I sure was out of place." She laughed. "I assure you, I'll never look at or eat sweet potatoes again without being reminded of that experience."

"There's a lot of great people to help with these projects around the county. Lots of good stuff going on. Guess you know by now about all the agriculture and livestock."

"I'm learning. My friend who helped me get the job didn't go into a lot of details about agriculture being the leading industry. It was a shock to my system. I know about fishing, coming from Seattle. Spent time in Los Angeles. There's a lot of farming in Nappa Valley, especially the grapes for wineries. I just wasn't familiar with chickens or cattle, and the only sweet potatoes I ate came from the grocery store."

"Is this going to be a permanent move, or just a stop over in career advancement?"

"I don't know. There are a lot of aspects to take into consideration. You were at the livestock sale. Do you have cattle?"

"A few head. I have a little farm out east. It occupies my spare time. It'll be a nice layout when I retire. You need to drop by and let me show you around." He placed a hand over his hat and moved a finger around the felt brim. His eyes watched the finger movement, as if contemplating his next words. He took a long drink from the coffee cup. "Are you going to the Farm City Banquet? It's a great place to meet a lot of the folks that make up the rock-solid foundation in this county."

Now, she hesitated. *Oh no. Is he going to ask me to go with him?* She had not pursued a social life since she arrived in North Fork. Most of her time had been devoted to becoming acquainted with the county. Her social calendar was a blank page, so maybe it was time to make a change.

"I may have to work it."

For a second his mouth opened as if wanting to say something, but it closed just as fast and he downed his last swig of brew.

"I've got to haul these potatoes out to the Owens place. I got the coffee," he said and started to slide out of the booth. She sensed a mood change. He paused and kept his attention on the hat in his hands. "Maybe we'll see you at the banquet. How about I check in with you later to see if you're going. What's your telephone number?"

She wrote it down for him, settled back in the booth, and watched as he made his way to the pickup, not fully understanding the confusion she felt in his wake. He wanted to say something, but stopped short before the words came out of his mouth.

In the next letter to Bruce, she may include the fact her null-and-void social life could be in for a change.

CHAPTER 6

She could hear the phone ringing from inside her apartment as she approached the wooden door. Her feet went into overdrive to cover the remaining steps on the tiled entrance and unlock the door. *I'm coming. Don't hang up.* Her fingers wrapped around the receiver.

"Hello."

"Hey, Caron. It's Bruce, kiddo. Thought I might catch you at home."

Excitement from hearing his voice filled her with a comfort as warm as the cup of hot chocolate and foamy marshmallows she looked forward to having later in the evening. She flopped into the recliner and pressed her toes against the heel of each foot to remove her shoes, then lifted her legs to sink onto the cushioning.

"It's so good to hear your voice. I miss you and all my friends."

"Kiddo, we miss you, too. So, how's it going?"

"Well, I have to admit, it's been interesting. You didn't tell me this was such a big agriculture community. I'm learning all about cows and chickens."

Laughter erupted on the other end of the line. "With your personality, you should fit in like a glove. You've got the capability of stepping right in and doing well."

"Yeah, that's what I'm afraid of, this steppin' in thing. Came real close to that when I took pictures of the 4-H steer winners at the county fair. Now, that was an experience."

"You hang in there, kiddo," he chortled, and if he'd been standing there in front of her she would have given him a playful kick on the chin or punch his arm in retaliation for not giving her the full story on the county's agriculture environment.

"The main reason I called. It may be nothing, but my apartment was broken into and all the papers ransacked."

The grasp she had on the receiver became so tight her hand tingled. The exuberance at first hearing his voice was dashed by a sudden chill. She was transported from the comfort of her living room to California and confronted with the shadow of a faceless stalker. The invasion of her California residence and the emotional violation of privacy struck a deep chord of rage and resentment.

The swelling in her throat from the acid reflux forced a cloud of protesting vapors into her mouth, and held her voice to barely above a raspy whisper. "What are you saying?"

"We're not sure yet. But after it happened, I talked with the detective who's been handling the case. I wanted to give you a heads up. It may just be coincidental."

"When did it happen?"

"A week ago."

Her breathing accelerated. She remembered the night she left the newspaper building after she filed the fatal accident story and the awareness something was amiss.

"Was anything taken?"

"The stacked papers on my desk were strewn around,

but that is where I kept your letters. The officers made a report and didn't seem to think it was relevant to your case but I wanted to let you know. I want you to stay on your toes."

She could not speak. An ominous silence crept into the room.

"Caron?"

"I'm here." Anxiety in her chest turned to an ache as more fear made the contents of her stomach boil in protest.

"Kiddo, I know the possibilities are so far-reaching it is unthinkable. You're three thousand miles away. But you just need to be alert. I'm not calling to upset you. You're my friend and I care about you."

"I'll be careful. Surely this dude wouldn't think about following me across the country. That's beyond comprehension. But I'll stay aware of my surroundings."

"So, how's everything else going?"

She was ready to redirect the conversation. "Good. I'm learning my way around the county. The folks at the newspaper office are real friendly. There's a big difference in small community and LA lifestyles."

"How about your social life? Met anyone interesting?"

She wasn't in the mood to pursue this part of the conversation at length, but did say, "Maybe. I don't know. I'll probably go to this Farm City Banquet thing. Seems to be a pretty big event here. A few people I know will be there. And you know how it is being the newest employee, catching all the nighttime assignments for a time period." She was not going to mention Bill.

"Caron, I think it was a good decision for you to make the change, not only for your emotional well-being, but also not being able to identify this weirdo puts you at risk."

"I know, and I appreciate your help."

"Well, just remember, you keep tabs on what's going on

around you, and I'm going to follow up in a few days to check on you again. You're going to take care? Right?"

"Absolutely. Thanks, Bruce. I'll be careful. We'll talk again soon."

She stared at the receiver so long the high, thin irritating sound, and the tinny operator saying, "if you'd like to make a call, please hang up and try again," interrupted the quiet. A new crop of disturbing possibilities packed up and moved back into her thoughts. She hung up the phone.

Its sudden ringing again caused her whole body to jerk in protest. *Maybe Bruce calling back.* Her fingers stopped their faint tremble when she lifted the receiver and answered.

"Hello, Bruce?"

"This is Bill Bonner, Caron. I was hoping I'd catch you home. Have I called at a bad time?"

"Oh, Bill. No. It's fine. I was talking to a friend back home, and thought he was calling back."

There was a long moment of silence. "Are you free for lunch tomorrow?"

The light tone of his words should have soothed her negative thoughts, but her mind still struggled to make its way back from the conversation with Bruce. "Sure, Bill. Okay."

"Is something wrong, Caron?"

"No. I'm sorry, Bill. My mind isn't working on all cylinders this evening. Let's meet at the North Fork Café. Noontime?"

"Whatever you want. So, we'll see you then. Uh, did you have a tough day?"

"It was busy. How about you?"

"I just finished my shift and turned in the report. It's a good day when nothing happens."

"That's great for a state trooper, isn't it?"

"I like quiet days, although riding around for hours can be

sort of boring. It beats responding to accidents and writing up traffic violations. Well, we'll see you at the café tomorrow."

"I'll look forward to it," she said.

She sat very still after hanging up the phone, reached for a throw pillow, clasped it to her chest, and dropped her chin onto its soft edging. Was the reprieve, moving to North Fork, over? Maybe. The stalker might not be in North Fork on a physical basis, but he'd gotten into her mind again, and she was by herself. At least she had Bruce when she lived in California. There had not been that much time to court close friendships since her arrival.

There was Barbara. But what would she think if Caron went to her with such a story. She couldn't involve anyone in North Fork. *Oh, it's silly. Everything is going to be all right.*

After all, it had been a good day, attending an extension office luncheon with Barbara to meet some of the county club presidents, and Sherry whom she had met at the community work day event was also present. Barbara did not act surprised when she told her that Bill had asked her to lunch.

"Bill's a good man. He's alone. You're alone. I know he's shown no permanent interest in anyone—saw him once or twice out for dinner, and we're around him regularly at the agricultural and livestock events. He's the kind of man you want on your side. Besides, we like you and want to keep you in North Fork."

"I don't know about that. All I'm trying to do is get a handle on this new lifestyle and do a good job. You've been a great help in getting me started."

Caron had accused Barbara of playing cupid, but the words she said, "Bill is the kind of man you want on your side," remained with her the rest of the evening as she made a sandwich, took a shower, and parked in the leather recliner to watch a little TV before bedtime.

Just before she said her evening prayer a new image formed in her thoughts. Bill. As the night wore on and she tossed one way, then the other, his presence grew stronger. When she was awake enough to hear the coffee pot and its steamy puffing sounds, she had decided when the time was right she'd broach the subject with him as to why she had moved to North Fork, maybe Barbara first. After a good cup of coffee under her belt, and on the way to the office she thought maybe they could share confidences, and promised to write Bruce that evening a note bringing him up-to-date with her activities.

By eleven-thirty she had caught up with the stories she'd been working on and heard the grumbling sounds in her stomach. The picture of a chili hotdog and cheese fries kept popping in her mind, along with the fact it was her first social meeting. She was indulging in the images that were beginning to appear like a sinfully tasty dessert.

She was sitting in the booth waiting when Bill pulled the trooper car into the lot, and she could see him with a radio microphone in his hand. He stood beside the closed door, and did not move, his head slightly atilt to stare out at the traffic. *What's wrong? Why is he waiting?* Then there was the abrupt movement she'd seen before, as if he were unsure and then with a made-up mind hurried along. His pace stretched into decisive long strides toward the café entrance.

I hope this is not a mistake.

The smallest smile played on his lips when his eyes found her, then sidled toward the booth. From the top of his head, minus the trooper hat to the shiny black patent shoes, he cut quite a figure; dark blue pants and matching jacket, lighter blue uniform shirt, all crisp and creased. Even the tie that matched the pants and jacket was perfectly placed, held by a clip with the emblem of the American flag.

The intensity she observed on his face as he stood beside the patrol vehicle and looked out on the traffic softened by the time he entered the café and was replaced with a slight upturn of his lips.

"This your day for hot dogs?"

She was gazing at the very noticeable, colorful state patch, "We Dare to Defend our Rights," on the shoulder of his uniform jacket. He removed it and she was treated to a view of bulging biceps in his arms. When he sat down in the booth, the shiny black belt that encircled a tapered waist squeaked leather on vinyl. He slid toward the middle and they were face-to-face. The sound had been pleasantly unnerving.

The waitress took their order, and then he turned his full attention to her.

"These are the best hot dogs I've ever eaten," she said. "There's an old timey diner in Van Nuys where I had occasion to eat and these remind me of home. But I think I mentioned that."

"I believe you said Seattle was your home."

Oops. "Oh, that's where it all began, and my parents still live there. I spent time in Los Angeles after getting my journalism degree."

"Is Caron Kimble your real name?"

Now, why did he ask that? She wasn't ready to cope with any explanation this soon, but there may be no choice.

"It's a byline name for privacy. There's nothing unusual about a journalist taking a pseudonym. In some places it's standard operating procedure." *I hope that explanation is sufficient.*

"So what's your real name?"

"Only for you and tax purposes—Caron Stallings."

When their food was placed on the table, to cover the pause in conversation, she pulled napkins from the dispenser and put them beside her plate. She was aware of his eyes searching her face as she squeezed ketchup from the plastic dispenser onto the fries.

"Ketchup on cheese fries?"

"I like ketchup. On everything."

His laugh helped to ease the nervous tension created when he asked about her name. She had spoken the truth without revealing the major reason for the change. *It's not time yet.*

"Tell me about this Farm City Banquet," she said, although Barbara had already filled her in on the event. She needed to talk about something. "Since I'm the newest employee looks like I draw the short straw. I'll be covering it for the paper."

"It's one of the biggest events of the year. One of our county producers is named Farm Family of the Year. It's quite an honor."

"Well, this will be my first."

"How do you like North Fork?" he asked.

"I'm settled. Barbara at the extension office has been so much help. She's taken me under her wing. It has been a tremendous help, and an interesting adventure."

"Adventure? That seems to indicate you may not make North Fork a permanent residence."

"Permanent is only a word. How long have you lived here?"

"Going on three years."

"Is it a permanent address for you?"

"It looks to be. I drove through North Alabama several years ago on the way to a job in West Virginia. I fell in love with the landscape, and at the time decided if the job didn't work out I'd get back here and see what was available."

The next question popped out before she could contain it.

She cursed her journalistic nosiness to ask questions. "Why did you leave West Virginia?"

She knew instinctively it was the wrong question. Storm clouds gathered in his eyes and the silence in his voice screamed her mistake in judgment. *Me and my big mouth.*

He stopped eating and moved sideways in the seat. She thought he was going to get up and leave. His eyes settled and cleared before he spoke. "There were some changes in my life." The tone in the sentence and its inflection of finality was her notice not to pry. *Change topics quick.*

"I can understand why the news department reports on depressing events. You see them, too, almost on a regular basis. How do you cope with it?"

He responded instantly to her change in conversation.

"We never get accustomed to it. I always like to feel my presence will make someone think the next time they speed, or act foolishly."

"That's a totally awesome responsibility. I admire law enforcement officers, and the role you all fill within the community. I'm not saying that just because you're sitting at this table. I'm sure there are aspects of your job the public never sees. I'll never forget a scene on the side of the highway one time. It's one of those things you never forget."

"Want to tell me about it?"

"I was going to an interview and saw some flickering lights ahead on the opposite side of the road and slowed down. There were officers all over the place, and this man down on his knees with his hands clasped behind his head. An officer was standing there pointing a gun right at the man. I've never seen anything like that."

"Sometimes circumstances call for drastic measures."

"I know. That's a side of life most of us don't ever see."

"Reality is not always a pretty picture," he said.

"You're right there." She popped the last cheese fry in her

mouth and chewed. "I've got to get back to work—have an afternoon appointment."

She moved to the edge of the seat and rose to leave. He did the same and reached for the check.

"Thanks for the lunch."

"Well, it's not a lot to thank me for. I feel guilty for us not going to one of the bigger restaurants."

"Don't. I happen to like hot dogs." She laughed and it seemed to please him.

"You like steak?"

"My second favorite food next to hot dogs."

"We'll set up a night for dinner."

"That sounds like fun. I'll look forward to it." She stopped beside her vehicle and he opened the door.

"Talk to you soon," he said, and headed to the patrol car.

She backed out of the parking spot and pulled her car onto the street, angling it to get a clear view of oncoming traffic. There was no preparing for what happened next. Her hand flew to the back of her head to stop the chilling sensation and cover the neck hairs standing on end. Her eyes scanned right, and left, then into the rearview mirror. *What is it?* Everything looked normal, even Bill's state patrol car behind her car. However, there was no preventing the creepy sensation that stayed with her the rest of the afternoon.

CHAPTER 7

Bill pulled off the leather gloves, one finger at a time. His movement was slow as if mulling over a decision to venture on. He crammed them in a side pocket on his denim jacket. The frayed straw hat was pulled so low on a smooth forehead it touched his eyebrows and thwarted any presence of the late afternoon sun.

He conceded the hat was beyond tattered and needed to be thrown away. Even the edging around the back of the brim had deteriorated into nothing more than protruding straw sticks. However, he did not have a wasteful bone in his body. Every time he cast an eye toward the trash can as the hat's final resting place, he changed his mind and abided by the half-hearted promise, "well, maybe I'll wear it one more time." It had been a year since he first made the half-hearted promise but he still preferred it to any of the others on the top shelf in his bedroom closet.

He hooked a boot heel on the bottom rail of the fence, folded his arms across his chest, and allowed his shoulders and hips to press against the remaining two boards. Long fingers rubbed over a scruffy day's growth of beard. It was his off day and shaving wasn't on his list of priorities.

Token lay near his feet, stretched out on her stomach, eyes alert for any ever-so-slight move to indicate a round of play. Her tail twitched as she waited for him to speak. He did nothing. She placed her chin on her front paws and sighed so deeply a thin vapor of dust was disturbed on the ground.

"Pretty girl, maybe I moved too fast, but shucks, it was only lunch. So, why do I feel out of sorts. I had the audacity to mention going out to dinner."

Token's head lifted in response to hearing her master's voice.

Bill removed the heel of his boot from the railing and squatted, his butt resting on the thick edge of the bottom board. His hand massaged as it dug deep into the fur on Token's neck. Her tail changed from a twitch to a solid thump.

"You didn't know me way back when, pretty girl. I had quite a reputation as a ladies' man, and wasn't patient when I saw something I wanted. Katherine changed all that. Hm. I reckon people might think I'm goofy sitting here talking to a dog." Token raised her head and issued a soft bark. He continued the massage. "You're a good girl and don't make any demands. All you want is to be fed, have water, and be loved. And I do love you, sweet baby. You've been good for me."

In another thirty minutes, dusk would force him to go into the house. This continued to be his favorite time of day, late afternoon when the world started to settle down for the night. The silence made room for memories of Katherine and he allowed images the full freedom to drift into his conscious thinking and meld with his desire to be with her again. The joy of her presence in his life had made him a happy man. He loved to watch the light bounce off her kinky red curls when she traipsed near. Only when he saw the mischievous glint in her eyes would his eyes move from her hair to her lips.

If it had not been for his friends, Allen and Pat, he would not have survived. They put up with his black moods and cynical outlook for a year. He had buried himself into working on Truck every night. Sometimes he forgot to eat for days. Pat sat him down and read him the riot act.

She told him she and Allen were going to be parents and, if it was a girl, they wanted to name her Katherine and call her Kat. He had cried and hugged Pat as if to hang onto his last hope for survival. He decided for his sanity he would leave Mason Springs. It had been the right decision. With his experience in law enforcement and military background it was no problem getting a job.

Soft pressure against his leg brought him back to the present from the trip down memory lane. He exhaled a deep sigh. "Token, I really enjoy being near Caron. I feel good when she's close."

The color of hazel-brown eyes slipped unhindered into his thoughts and he saw his reflection in the depths of those twin pools. They were Caron's eyes. He wanted to get even closer to see if those luminous flecks of gold actually existed or if they were a figment of his imagination. What was it he had read about eye colors? People with brown eyes were naturally creative. Caron was certainly in the right profession. He couldn't remember much more, but there was something about individuals with brown eyes having enduring strength and a humble spirit. He discarded those last couple of words, wanting nothing to do with anything spiritual, still questioning *why* someone as good as Katherine had to die.

He rose from the squatting position and leaned forward to stretch the cramped muscles in his legs. "Come on, girl."

Token was up in a heartbeat. "Let's go in." Together, they walked toward the house in the gathering darkness. With each step came the awareness he wanted to know everything about Caron Kimble, or Caron Stallings? Whatever. He thought he understood. She was a woman alone. He was alone. He'd actually asked if she wanted to go out for dinner.

When her lips spread and changed from a smile into a soft pucker of thought, he was shocked at himself, wanting to soothe a need to kiss that mouth. He wanted to make her lips swell with passion. He subdued the arousing thought, but not the impending possibility. Maybe he'd invite her out to his farm and show her around. After all, it was the friendly thing to do.

"Do you think she might want to come out and take a look, pretty girl. She said she likes steak." This time there was no mistaking the excited bark from Token. "Yeah, I said a magic word, didn't I, pretty girl?"

* * *

CARON WELCOMED the beckoning light in the apartment complex foyer. Her appointment for a five o'clock photo shoot at city hall turned out to be a late arrival. So, it was after six o'clock and she came home in the dark. When the sun went down she wanted to be in her living room, behind locked doors, a holdover from the shadowy fears in Los Angeles. The joy she experienced seeing a beautiful sunset had turned to dislike with the possibility of a lurking stalker.

Her excitement could hardly be contained when she opened the mail slot and saw the letter from Bruce. She couldn't wait and tore into the letter before she got inside the apartment.

She started to read as her foot pushed to close the door behind. Her free hand turned the lock on the knob. Not even the final echo of metal against metal when the dead bolt slid into place took her attention from the letter.

HI KIDDO,

I wasn't trying to upset you when I called and told you someone broke into my apartment. The police still don't have any clue, and I can't find anything missing. My desk had been ransacked and papers strewn all over the floor. They think it was a random act of vandalism.

It's this feeling I don't like that keeps hanging around. This sounds ridiculous, but I can't help it.

You be careful and keep your eyes open. If I find out anything different about the break-in, you'll know first.

Have you met anyone yet?
Take care of yourself and I'll be in touch soon.
Bruce

HER HUNDRED AND thirty pounds felt like a ton of weight, too much for her legs. She sagged into the recliner so hard air whooshed from the cushion and interrupted the heavy silence. The letter remained on her lap.

Why me, Lord?

The wide, plate glass, living room window yawned its indifference. She bolted upright and ran to pull the Venetian blind cord, wanting to shut out any menace that toyed with her mental stability. The quiet became oppressive. Her body reacted and flashes of heat ran wild patterns over her skin. Sweat started to build in the crevices on each side of her nose, and she lifted both hands to wipe it away.

At that moment she felt vulnerable and open to attack. She grabbed a throw pillow and hugged it tight against her heaving breasts and tried to calm her breathing. *Breathe,*

Caron. Slow down and breathe. Her head bowed and she closed her eyes. When they opened again, her lips parted and she said, "amen."

As her breathing became even again, she stopped hugging the pillow so tightly, and let it fall onto her lap. However, she placed her hands, palms down, on the cushion, slid them back and forth, and rubbed at the silk material much like a cat sharpening its claws, but in her case the motion was to calm rampant emotions. She had promised to write Bruce. Perhaps now would be the time, needing to stay busy.

She walked into the bedroom and got a pad and pen from the dresser drawer. Her stomach growled a demand for food. However, she sat back down in the recliner and started to write. Her hand poised over the note pad hesitated.

Again, she asked, "why me, Lord?" She was far from being perfect, but tried to follow the advice, "Do unto others as you would have them do unto you." Her parents had taken her to church at an early age, and she had been taught and accepted the belief of "love thy neighbor" and "thou shalt not steal" and all the other commandments. So, why should she not ask the Lord, "why me?" Almost in an instant she felt remorse for her insolence. "Who am I to question?" she pondered aloud, and chastised herself to get off the pity post and write the darn letter. The pen in her hand wrote the first two words. Her mind cautioned to keep the theme light for the time being.

Dear Bruce,

Our minds are working on the same wavelength. There have been times when I get a creepy feeling, and then consider it silly.

Funny you should ask if I've met anyone. I went to lunch with someone I met when I volunteered for a community project. By the way, he's a state trooper. His name is Bill Bonner. I had first met him when I had to cover a vehicle accident.

He mentioned going out to dinner.

Yes, I will stay vigilant. But LA and the past are three thousand miles away.

Take care and we'll talk again soon.

Caron

SHE SEALED the envelope and placed it beside her purse to mail the following day. Her stomach issued another rolling protest and she hurried to the kitchen. A ham and cheese sandwich and glass of milk would quiet her innards. A smile lifted her lips as she piled on the ham and cheese, kosher dill pickles, and the tangy sandwich spread. She added a few sour cream and onion chips to the plate and hurried back down to the recliner. Her thoughts drifted to Bill.

There was something about him that spoke volumes of his quiet strength. Taking the first bite, she remembered the strong arms, flat stomach, narrowed waist, and powerful thighs. Suddenly she couldn't breathe.

The phone rang. It jarred her images of Bill as she picked up the receiver.

"Hello."

"Caron—Bill Bonner."

The incoming call lightened her mood.

"Hey, I have a thought," he said. "How about you come out to the farm this Saturday? I've got to check out a calf at Matthew's. He's a friend I do business with, but I'll do that early morning. When you get here we'll trek around on the UTV. I'd enjoy taking you on a little tour. And you'll meet Token."

"Token?"

"I'll tell you the story, and grill you a good steak. I cook up a fine T-bone. You said steak was your second favorite food next to hot dogs."

The sound of his laughter through the phone line filled her spirit with new hope. "That sounds like loads of fun. What can I bring?" He'd made it so easy to accept the invitation.

"Nothing but a healthy appetite. I have everything—two o'clock. That'll be plenty of time to take you around the place and then I'll cook up those steaks."

"Healthy appetite I got," she said. "I'll look forward to meeting Token, and having steak."

"Well, then, we'll see you Saturday."

"Fantastic. All I need is directions."

"It's easy to find," he said. "Got paper and pen?"

"I do now," she said, ready to write.

His directions were thorough and detailed. She was familiar with most of the road numbers he named.

"If I get lost, I'll call. Give me a number where you can be reached," she said.

After she had written down the number and they hung up, she finished her sandwich. She was walking the empty plate to the kitchen sink when the phone rang again.

Maybe he forgot to tell me something. She hurried to pick up the receiver.

"Hello."

There was a click and the line went dead.

Before she could get back to the kitchen to wash the plate, the phone rang again. Her steps scooted back into the living room, a bit of exasperation starting to show on her face.

"Hello," she said, and realized her voice was a little sharper.

Silence was her answer. She knew someone was on the other end, could hear a panting breath.

"Who's there? I don't have time to play games."

The menacing snigger that reverberated through the telephone line shook her to the core.

"I'm going to hang up," she said.

It wasn't fast enough. There was laughter, so loud it still made her earlobes vibrate with the receiver a good two feet away. She stared at the display—unavailable. The silence became so thick Caron believed she would suffocate. A reverberating dial tone made her jerk. Before she could even consider her next move, she was at the front door of the complex, gave it a sharp pull, and stepped outside. Her lungs filled with the fresh air she so desperately needed. She decided it was time to share her problem with Bill. But the timing had to be right, maybe Saturday.

* * *

She said it, "play games." If that's what she wanted to do, Dexter would oblige.

He managed to keep the exhilaration that swirled in his chest contained until he made it out of the library and sat down in the car. Trembling desire surged through his body, a response to merely hearing her voice.

Congratulations were in order. When he got into her friend's apartment and found letters from Caron on the desk, the name she used in the North Fork newspaper was an open, blatant invitation to find her. There were even telephone numbers. It had been so easy. All the information he needed was right there for the taking.

She made the game interesting and he knew the reward for his efforts would be worthwhile. He would make love to her and she would scream in ecstasy.

The telephone call was just to let her know he was near.

I understand, my darling. I'll come to you when the time is right—when there's no longer a reason to continue the chase. You'll be mine to love forever. Be patient, my darling.

He started the car and drove in the direction of the North Fork Café. He would sit in the same seat she occupied when she was with that state trooper. Fate was on his side and would intervene. It would be empty and waiting. Instant hatred for the man in uniform caused his body to go stone-cold rigid. If it had not been for his low and deep-throated growl, the grinding of teeth may have been heard as he stared out at the street ahead.

His jealousy of the officer turned into a war of resentment. It eased for a second when he considered it was probably a meeting due to her job, but bounced back with vengeance to the forefront of his thoughts. He'd see to it there would be no meetings when Caron was his alone. He did not like the fact she worked because it would mean she had to be around men. She would not work. He'd see to that. Her only job would be to make him happy. He would make her his love slave.

For a moment he forgot about the call when an image of the officer ballooned in his thoughts and instant hatred was rejuvenated with a promise he'd thwart any interest. He would keep her a prisoner of love. When he showed her all he could offer, she would be willing to put aside all the worldly interests and live to placate his every desire.

CHAPTER 8

Caron considered all possible avenues of reason for the phone call. It may have been a prank, intended to be an obscene phone call. The stalker was three thousand miles away. *The chance he may know where I moved is so asinine.* Over the following days the despicable laugh she heard mellowed. Thoughts about the call dropped farther down her list of concerns. Saturday and the trip to Bill's farm induced more pleasant feelings.

Her state of mind was still upbeat at midday as she put on jeans and a sleeveless cotton blouse. Pronounced sunbeams on that fall day were welcomed, but she still deferred on the side of caution and got a jacket from the closet.

As she headed out of the city, her eyes scanned and appreciated the first hints of a seasonal change on the landscape. The countryside was dotted with small ponds. There must have been a light breeze, just enough to stir the surface waters. The sun was caught in the movement and its rays transformed to sparkles of light that danced and flickered across the water. *Wonder if Bill has a pond on his farm? 'Course, we haven't really talked about what he has and doesn't have.* The tour would answer her questions.

There was no sign of him when she drove up to the house. A moment of doubt played through her mind that she may have pulled into the wrong driveway. That was dismissed when she heard a motor and searched for its source. He was steering a utility vehicle in her direction and waving. She got out of the car and waved back. The closer he got, the higher her spirits soared.

"You had no problem finding the place?" he said, stopping the vehicle just a few feet away.

"The directions were perfect, and I enjoyed the drive."

"The steaks are marinating."

She stared in admiration at the trim, lithe physique and defined confidence in his stride as he closed the gap between them. It was hard to remain oblivious to his generous smile or watch the sunlight search his face and light up every detail from the glint of contentment in his eyes to the touch of humor on sensuous lips.

"There's a little hitch in plans." He explained the morning visit to Matthew's farm had been cancelled. He was called out of town for a family emergency.

"We'll reschedule it, and maybe you can go, too. I want you to meet them, especially his wife, Molly. They're good folks. What do you think?"

"Fine with me." Before she changed her mind, she said, "I'll look forward to it." She stepped in his direction but her progress was blocked.

"Token," he said in a calm voice, directing his attention to the dog that stood in her path. "She's a friend, pretty girl." The dog looked to Bill, then gave Caron a real once-over study before she ambled back to Bill's side.

"Ready?" he asked. "Do you need something to drink before we take off?" He took a couple of strides. The air between them stirred. He was so near she had to look up to answer, and close enough to appreciate his fragrance of cedar and freshly mown hay.

"I'm good. Maybe a cup of coffee when we get back."

Token took a quick bounce ahead when they walked toward the vehicle. A leap, and she was in the middle of the front seat.

Bill's quiet chuckle had a distinct ring of embarrassment. "Token, mind your manners. We have a guest."

Caron laughed and got in beside her. "I don't believe there's any doubt where she's accustomed to riding." She was cautious, and made her next move in a manner as if it was something she did every day, no big deal. Her hand on Token's head caressed the soft, slick hair. Token responded and inched closer.

"I see you're winning her approval. She doesn't sidle up to strangers. Between the job and maintaining the farm there hasn't been many visitors, so she's not had a lot of contact with people.

Caron kept her attention on Token. "How long have you had her?"

"Found her in the corner of the barn one morning shortly after I bought this place. She was a scrawny pup, hurt and nearly starved."

Those words caused Caron to increase the pressure of her hand on Token's head from light to firm in an attempt to comfort and reassure the dog. "You found a forever home didn't you?" she said, bending closer, her voice almost a whisper in Token's ear. The response from the dog was instant. Her head tilted to the side and a cold nose brushed against Caron's cheek. She could see Bill's jawline relax in an expression of satisfaction.

"I take her with me on short visits when she doesn't have to sit in the cab too long, but not in warm weather. Some-

ECHOES FROM THE MOUNTAIN

times she rides when I'm about the farm. Other times she lopes alongside. I leave it up to her."

He eased the UTV from the front yard to the back of the barn, stopping to open a gate, and steered the vehicle into an open field. Her hand remained on Token's head. A bump on the uneven ground lifted her off the seat. "Whee! Hold on, Token." She laughed and kept a hand on Token's head, but her arm went around Token to stabilize the dog. Caron was secure in a seat strap.

Bill glanced at both of them and grinned. "Everybody okay?"

He took a hand off the steering wheel to cover and squeeze hers in a protective gesture. The pleasant sensation spread a flash of warmth over her arm. He slowed the vehicle. She wanted to know why and when she lifted her chin to ask, she was face-to-face with a pair of chestnut brown eyes that crinkled with amusement. His expression was so reassuring she allowed herself to be captured in their depth.

He had just started to increase speed when he ran over something that made the vehicle careen and bounced her high in the seat. Her arm tightened around Token, and the hand that covered hers grabbed the steering wheel until their movement was stopped. Bill twisted in the seat to look back. "I didn't see that one." He tapped her on the shoulder. "See that?"

She angled her body to see what he was talking about. It was a mound camouflaged by an abundance of grass.

"Fire ant hill. They'll sneak up on you when you least expect them," he said.

"Fire ant hill? Do I need to know about them."

"They're all over the south—dangerous—will eat you alive. Producers say they've lost new born calves—seems the ants are drawn to the scent of a calf's birth. They'll cover and sting it to death. Don't let them get on you. Their bites can raise blisters."

"Oh, that's good to know." Mentally she was again going to lay into Bruce for not informing her about such infernal pests.

She was still berating Bruce in her mind when they reached the top of a small incline.

Bill stopped the vehicle and pushed back to stretched his long legs. He slid an arm across the top of the seats, the hand coming to a landing near the back of her neck, but he made no attempt to touch.

Ahead she saw movement on the far side of a stand of trees—cattle stirred and gazed at them. "They know the motor sound," Bill said, and pointed in their direction.

In the distance she could see a fair-sized pond, the waning afternoon sun reflecting an orange glow on the surface. "This must be a beautiful place at sunset."

"It is. I've spent a lot of time here. It's a great thinking place."

"Everyone needs a cubby hole for private thoughts. There was a city park in LA where I sat and watched children play. Their voices were muffled, but the sound was quietly reassuring. I had to give it up." She wasn't aware of her deep sigh until he made a half turn in the seat.

"Why did you give it up?"

The question sliced through the distance between them. Her thoughts scrambled for an answer. This was not the time or place to discuss the problem.

"Hmm—time. I allowed the job to take precedence. At the end of the day all I wanted to do was get home."

"I was lucky to get this farm. I lived in New Orleans, so I've had a taste of big city life—can't picture living off the farm now. Reckon this is where I'll retire,"

"Sounds like you have it all planned out."

"It'll require the right equipment, and more fencing—all in due time. Ready to move on?"

"I'm with you," she said.

By the time they maneuvered around the acreage and he stopped to check out a few feeding bins, longer evening shadows alerted them dusk wasn't far away. Bill flipped on the headlights and they headed back to the house.

"Hungry?"

"Not bad. I had a good lunch, but looking forward to that coffee."

"I'll brew you up a cup. I want you to have a good appetite for those steaks. The potatoes are in the oven. I set the timer right before you got here, and a fresh salad is covered and waiting in the fridge."

Her laughter filled the air. "Aren't you the smart one. I'll be looking forward to a taste of your culinary talents. By the time you get that steak ready, I'll have more than a good appetite."

The hum of the UTV motor didn't skip a beat on their way back. He pulled it inside the barn and the three of them got down from the high seats. They were in no hurry to get to the house, watching the sun dip lower on the horizon, allowing dusk its moment before dark claimed its rightful place.

"It's a beautiful evening," she said.

"I've been fortunate to see a lot of them right from the front yard."

They took a couple of steps onto the porch and she stood aside for him to open the door. She felt the brush of his hand against her lower back as he nudged her into a living room. Token was right on their heels.

"I'll get that coffee started. Make yourself at home."

"Can I help?"

"Won't take a jiffy, but you're sure welcome to come on out to the kitchen."

She fell in behind him as he led the way. Her delight could not be contained when he moved aside and she walked through the kitchen door.

"Now this is a kitchen," she said, moving deeper into the room and scanning both walls, her gaze ending at the cozy nook at the far end where windows encased three sides. When the sun rose surely it would engulf that end of the room with a bounty of light for the small table, a perfect fit for the space.

She leaned against the counter and watched his agile movements. He turned a knob on the oven and opened the door. Token jogged to the center of the room, plopped down on the tiled floor, and watched the activity.

"Potatoes are ready." Without stopping, he opened a cabinet and got a canister.

"There's so much space in here. Did you design it? The island in the center—perfect—plenty of room on all sides."

"It was all here when I bought the place. I put in appliances and the furniture. I was told the former owners had a large family. None of the heirs wanted to continue farming after their parents died."

"You have excellent taste," she said, admiring the stainless steel appliances conveniently positioned, the shiny surfaces making the room appear even brighter. Within no time he was filling two cups.

"How do you drink your coffee?"

"Cream and one sugar substitute if you have it."

He opened the fridge, pulled out a container, and a smaller canister from the cabinet. These were placed on the counter where she stood. The cup of coffee he handed her was so hot steam vapors drifted from the center.

"It smells so good." She took the first sip, closed her eyes, and let it slide down her throat. "Ah. You make good coffee."

"The coffee pot does all the work." He held his cup in one hand, crossed one ankle over the other and leaned a shoulder against the fridge. Each time he took a drink of his own coffee she could feel his eyes watching her over the rim of the cup.

"This is nice. Bill, I enjoyed the tour." She did not keep back the giggle. "Even hitting that fire ant hill."

"Sorry about that. I should have kept my mind on what I was doing."

"What *were* you thinking about?" She lowered her head, shocked at the blatant question and how fast it escaped her mouth. An embarrassed blush burned on her cheeks.

"I think the pretty lady sitting beside me diverted my attention."

CHAPTER 9

Caron wanted to kick herself for the words that slipped from her lips. There you go again. Mouth in action. Her mind scrambled for something to say, a rebuttal that would be playful yet cool the flame on her face and abstain from thinking he had meant his comment as a romantic inclination. Bill took the next step.

"Let's go to the living room and finish the coffee. It won't take long for those steaks to cook. It's such a nice evening I thought we might eat out on the patio?" He didn't skip a beat.

Her heart did. "I like that," she said.

She settled in a corner of the sofa and he sat down on the other end. As she lifted the cup to drink, her gaze drifted to the framed picture sitting on the coffee table.

"What a beautiful child."

"That little darling is the daughter of a very special friend. You should see *her* mother. She's a beauty, too. I just got it framed."

The words "very special friend" and "beauty, too" slammed her feminine ego at the possibility she may not be the only woman in his life. She took another sip of coffee to swallow her disappointment, but an inkling of what she was considering must have shown on her face.

"She's Pat and Allen's daughter, my very best friends in West Virginia. We keep in regular contact. They may be visiting in the spring. They call her Kat."

"Kat?"

This time when he spoke his voice changed and each word was velvet soft. "Her real name is Katherine, and yes, it's a nickname. She was named after my late wife. I called my wife Kat. We were very close with Pat and Allen, went through a lot together."

She said nothing. It would be up to him if he wanted to pursue the story of his wife's death. However, she held onto the feeling that something special, an understanding had passed between them in that moment.

"Ready to eat? I'll start the steaks."

"What can I do?" They both rose from the sofa and went toward the kitchen.

He paused a minute before his mouth lifted in a wide grin. "I'll get the steaks, take care of the potatoes. I'm going to grill the bread, too. How about bringing out the salad, all the stuff in the fridge, you know, butter, sour cream—plates and glasses are in the cabinet. We can do sweet iced tea, soft drinks, or water."

"I'll do water with a slice or squirt of lemon. Either will do. Whatever you have."

He continued to move around the kitchen, picked up a covered container from the counter, and carried it out to the patio, then came back for a tray of bread, thick round slices slathered in a generous helping of butter. "Oh, I put garlic powder on the bread. How do you like your steak?"

"Medium well. Can I fix your drink?"

"I'll do tea. That's one of the things I really missed living up north. Couldn't get a glass of sweet iced tea with a meal in a restaurant." Caron scrunched her mouth in a distasteful gesture. "They drink a lot of brewed herbal tea where I come from. I didn't like the taste of any of it."

She was glad he went back outside. It gave her a moment to think. He had shared private information about his past life. There was a tone of reverence in his voice when he spoke of his wife. The perceived trust he placed in her by sharing the knowledge was evident. He had made her feel at home by the nonchalant manner in which he accepted her offer to help with the meal preparation.

It took two more trips from the kitchen to the patio to get everything they needed, and by the time dinner plates were on the table, the teasing aroma from the grill was making her mouth water. He was busy at the grill and had his back to her, so she enjoyed a long look, and wondered how far this man's talents extended.

"I'm starved," she said, going to stand beside him.

He gave her a sideways glance and gave the steaks another turn. The pop of juices dropping onto charcoal promised of delights to come. The sounds were torture to her stomach.

"Steaks are ready. Bring the plates."

She didn't hesitate. They were still sizzling when she and Bill sat down at the table.

Token sat on quivering haunches and scooted closer to the table, licking her lips and issuing a soft whine of anticipation.

Caron watched her and laughed. "I know she's not that excited to be near me."

"Token, you'll have to wait. Now, be a good girl and lay down."

Token looked at Bill as he spoke, let out a big sigh and laid down, but she didn't give up her position. Two big brown eyes settled on Caron.

"She's going to plead her case to you, Caron."

"Well, the jury's back and she won. I won't forget you, Token, but I get the first bite."

Bill's laughter filled the air around them. "She does this to me anytime I sit down to eat."

Caron turned her attention back to the steak, cut into the meat, and ferried the morsel to her mouth. Her tongue absorbed the first juices and made the rest of her senses come alive. She chewed and savored, her stomach clamoring for more.

She could barely talk, wanting all her energy invested in chewing each delectable bite, but the expectant look on Bill's face made her pause. "I've never tasted steak this good. What did you marinate them in?"

"Secret's in the sauce, but between you and me, I add a little Jack Daniels bourbon," he said, pleased with her approval.

She broke off a piece of toasted bread and sopped it in the extra sauce that seeped from the steak to the edge of her plate.

"Token?" A head quickly rose. "Girl, you'll get the bone, but I may gnaw it first."

This time Bill's laughter rang with the sound of satisfaction. "You like your steak."

"You can cook me one anytime you want."

"Only if you come out here for the meal."

Caron didn't gnaw the bone as she had promised Token, but she did carve off every taste of meat possible, and with a baked potato topped with butter and sour cream, plus the salad, her stomach was firmly packed.

Bill finished eating and gave Token the bone which she held between her paws and totally ignored them both as she gnawed and chewed until Caron called her name. Token left the bone she had ravaged and took the one Caron offered.

"She's happy," Bill said.

"Come on," Caron said. "I'll help you clear the table, and we'll get these dishes washed."

"We'll put them in the dishwasher," he said.

That chore was completed in no time. They went back into the living room, and this time Caron didn't ease onto the sofa, rather sort of plopped into the cushioning and slid back, extended and stretched her legs.

"That's the best meal I've ever had." She looked up at him.

"Let me refresh our coffee." he said.

"I'll make room for it." She patted her full tummy. "Can I help?"

"Won't take a sec. Stay comfortable."

"No argument from me. Me and my tummy are happy *right* here." She could hear the chuckle that vibrated his shoulders as he went toward the kitchen.

Now she noticed the room. It was cozy, the furniture in muted tones of tan and brown. It was a rather large room. A high ceiling dated the house before the 1950s and it wouldn't have surprised her if the rock in the fireplace hadn't come from adjacent fields. The room had several double windows, one on each side of the front door. The room would be well lit with windows decorating the opposite walls. She wondered if the reasoning was to allow lots of light to beam through the glass panes. There was a photo album on the end of the coffee table and her curiosity wanted to take a peek, but didn't dare. He had trusted her with a bit of his past. She'd wait until he invited her back in for more.

His steps were more calculated when he walked back into the room with a coffee cup in each hand. He kept his attention on them until he handed her one and sat down, a little closer this time.

He watched as she settled deeper into the cushions, contented at the first sip from the cup.

"How about going with me to the Farm City Banquet. It's next week. I'll be working the night shift, but off Friday." The question was simple and direct. He drank from his cup and waited for her answer.

"I've been assigned the event. That means I'll be taking pictures and moving around. I'm the newest staff member so I draw more of the night assignments. Do you mind?"

"Of course not. You have a job to do. Pat, Allen's wife—the friends I mentioned—she's a reporter. That's how I first met her. I was a deputy sheriff and she came by the courthouse to get information on a story she was working."

"Did she work in the news department?"

"Well, actually, no. She was out on a public relations assignment and got caught up in a news story."

Caron emptied the last sip of coffee. "Hmm. Bill, this has been a wonderful evening, but I need to get back to the apartment. I go to nine o'clock church services. That means I'm up early. Do you have a home church?"

He tilted the cup to finish off his coffee. "I haven't decided on one." There was a slight hesitation in his demeanor.

After living and working in the county for more than two years. Something's not right.

"Then I'll invite you to attend church some Sunday with me."

"Maybe. We'll see. By the way, I need your address."

"I live in the Wild Woods Apartments. Funny—not a tree on the grounds. Across the street, but nothing around the apartments. It's downstairs, number two." She also gave him her cell phone and apartment numbers. You can catch me at one of these."

She rose and he helped her put on her jacket. His hands lingered at the back of her neck as she felt him straighten her collar. He walked her to the car and opened the door.

"That steak was cooked perfect." She angled her head in a

cockish position to the side and gazed directly in his face. "And the sauce was so good. Couldn't resist sopping it on that piece of bread."

She started to get in the car.

"Just a minute."

"What?"

He put a hand under her chin, and nudged it so she had to look directly into his face, then to the side. "The napkin didn't get all the sauce."

Her hand started toward her face, but he stopped it with his.

"I'll get it for you." He leaned into her and his lips covered the corner of her mouth.

She felt the tip of his tongue glide against her skin. Rockets ignited and lifted her to heights that promised a journey to the moon. The lunar trip ended too soon when he stopped and took a step back. Her face burned with the unexpected heat of passion. She regained enough strength to put a step of distance away from the mounting inferno she felt radiating off his body. An expression of shocked revelation on his face almost took her breath away.

He started to speak, but hesitated and swallowed first. "Call me when you get home. I want to know you arrived safe."

All her voice could allow was, "Okay." She started the car and was halfway down the drive when it occurred to her there hadn't been a speck of sauce on her mouth. Bill Bonner's expertise wasn't all confined to the kitchen. His creative talents were also appreciated. A giggle filled the silence inside her vehicle.

When she pulled into her parking spot at the apartment complex it was only then she realized there was no memory of driving back to North Fork. Bill's laid-back demeanor had put her at a comfortable level accepting his invitation to the banquet. Her trembling fingers moved to the corner of her mouth where his lips and tongue had pressed against her skin. Any doubt was alleviated.

What do they say about people with brown eyes? Where had that thought come from, she asked herself, still sitting in the car, and making no move to get out. She answered her own question. *I read somewhere the character of the person is grounded in deep connection to nature, the earth, and their personalities exuded strength.*

A silent confession filled her mind. He aroused her emotionally and physically, and she wanted his strength.

CHAPTER 10

The evening she had anticipated arrived. It was not the Farm City event itself, but going to the banquet with Bill that caused the pleasant tickle in her tummy. Having an evening out in the company of a gentleman, even if she would have to share him with several hundred people, had her skipping through the day to complete assigned tasks. Bill said there would be lots of friendly folks attending the event and it would be an opportunity for her to meet some of the county producers.

She glanced at the clock on the TV when she heard the knock. He was on time. When she opened the door, her eyes feasted on the most gorgeous man she had ever seen. From the lapels on his denim suit jacket to the straight-legged jeans and spit-polished boots, he was an apparition most women only dream about. Her mouth went dry and a tongue normally ready to speak intelligent sentences clamped tight to the roof of her mouth.

"Ready?"

She had to lick her lips and swallow twice to wet her mouth before she could answer.

"Need to get my purse and camera," she said, and made a quick move to the sofa to cover her embarrassment for the steady gaze. He had looked fine in a trooper uniform, but dressed in denim from top to bottom was a sight that would make any red-blooded American woman drool. She actually felt a little dowdy in her skirt and blazer. Being a representative of the newspaper mandated her choice of attire.

"You look nice," she said to break the silence.

"It's been a while since I've been in dressy clothes. I'm partial to old jeans. You always look great."

When he opened the door to the apartment complex foyer, her gaze landed on Truck, parked next to her vehicle.

"Hope you don't mind going in Truck—had to take the SUV in for a maintenance check. They wanted to keep it overnight."

"Are you kidding? I've never ridden in a classic like this—seen them at antique shows, but never an opportunity to ride in one. This is a treat." She hurried to the passenger's side with him hot in her wake and had the door open before he could reach the handle. Her advance was stopped cold when she scrutinized the height from the pavement to the seat. She considered how much height she could manage in the confines of her skirt.

"I'm sorry. I didn't think about that." His laugh was soft. "You're the first woman to ride in Truck. Let me give you a hand."

"I got this," she said, tossing her clutch purse and placing the camera satchel on the floorboard. Using her left hand, she lifted the hem of her skirt and held it above her knee. She gripped the top of the open door with the other and planted a foot on the side step. The firm hand she felt under her elbow remained until she was seated. Before she could look up and thank him, he was already making long strides to his side.

The touch of his hand on her elbow left a tingle on her skin and that rattled her for a moment. She needed to say something to calm the intense spurts of pleasure darting across her chest. "I can see everything from the front seat of a truck," she said, keeping her focus straight ahead.

She knew what was going to happen next, watched, and giggled as his hands remained on the steering wheel and the motor started.

"I can see how that would freak out folks," she said, knowing his foot pressing on a floorboard pedal had started the engine. "That is just too cool."

"Have you had a good week?" He talked as he backed Truck out of the parking spot and onto the street. His movement stirred the air in the cab and an earthy musk aroma teased her nostrils.

The telephone calls skittered through her mind, but the reminder was dismissed. *The timing has to be right.* She didn't want a negative shadow to cross what promised to be a nice evening.

"Pretty routine. How about you?"

"Same here. Did lots of riding and had less paper work."

It was only a few blocks to the civic center. As they approached, he slowed Truck and scanned the parking lot. "Good thing we came on early. Looks like it's going to be an overflow crowd."

The first person she saw entering the building was Barbara. When she spotted them, her face lit up like a bonfire on a fall evening before a pep rally. She hurried from behind a table where she was collecting tickets and made a beeline in their direction.

"Two of my favorite people, and together. Caron—Bill. Lordy, this makes my evening." She pulled Caron to the side while Bill handed his ticket to the other woman seated at the table.

Caron was close enough to hear Barbara's feverish whisper. "Girl, ya'll look good together."

"Barbara, this is nothing but a friendly social outing. So, no playing cupid stuff, you hear? This banquet is my assignment for the night."

"Well, it's time you started getting out."

"Getting out where?" Bill interjected as he walked up and heard the tail end of the conversation.

"I was just telling Caron, it's good to see ya'll. Lord knows Caron has kept her nose to the grindstone, and you, Bill, it's been ages since I've seen you out for an evening other than business."

"Well, we'll just see if we can't change that," he said, and made a playful wink at Caron as he tucked her elbow into his hand and nudged her toward the open double doors. Caron was about to ask him what he meant when he grinned and said, "Funning her. That should keep her thinking for a spell. Hope you didn't mind."

When she saw a dancing light in his eyes she kept her responsive giggle silent, and said, "That was mean, Bill."

"Nah. Give her something to talk about. I know her."

Caron was seeing a fun side to him, and relished the discovery.

"Where do you want to sit?" He continued to escort her deeper into the auditorium. Dozens of long tables, covered in pristine white tablecloths, were filling up fast.

"As close to the front as possible—easier to get photos. We may have to stay a little while after the dinner to get a picture of the farm family. Hope you don't mind."

"No problem." He nudged her to a couple of empty chairs. When they were seated, she placed her purse and camera bag between her feet under the table, and made a scan of the surroundings. An unfamiliar voice interrupted her concentration.

"Bill. Good to see you. How you doing, buddy?"

Caron turned and watched the stranger's hand clap Bill on the shoulder, and the firm handshake between the two of them. She recognized him as one of the men Bill had been talking to at the livestock barn.

"Matt. Doing just fine. Family here?"

"Just me and Molly tonight. She's sitting over there," he said and pointed.

Bill looked until he found her and waved. His lips spread into a wide grin when she returned the wave. Caron had also searched the crowd and found Matt's wife. She smiled and nodded in Molly's direction and a happy expression acknowledged the greeting.

"Hey, buddy. That calf we talked about is near weaned. She's going to be a real good investment. Sorry I had to skip out on you the other day. How's this Saturday to come over? We'll take care of the details."

"Thanks. I'll do that. Matt, do you know Caron Kimble with the *Daily News*?"

He extended his hand to Caron. "Seen her articles in the paper. I'm Matthew Harrison. Nice to meet you in person."

"It's nice to meet you," she said.

"Anytime Saturday good for you?" Bill asked.

Matthew grinned. "My entire day is going to be spent at the house. I don't really have a choice. Molly says she's going to can apples and volunteered me to help with toting them into the house."

Bill laughed. "Good for Molly."

"This Saturday," he said. "About nine?"

Bill turned to Caron. "Nine Saturday morning okay with you?"

She hesitated for only a second. "Yes. I won't be in the way, will I?"

ECHOES FROM THE MOUNTAIN

"Are you kidding? No way," Bill said, and turned back to Matthew. "We'll see you Saturday morning."

When Matthew returned to sit beside Molly, Bill faced her and crossed his arms on the table. "Matt and Molly are great folks, and good neighbors."

"I'm looking forward to Saturday. Bill, I need to get a couple of crowd photos. Be right back," she said and reached for the camera. She headed to the front of the auditorium and side stage steps to give her the height she needed to show the huge crowd. When she returned, the food had arrived.

It turned out to be a good evening. Even the cold mashed potatoes and chicken went down well. After the events concluded, she made the necessary pictures of the Farm Family of the Year. She glanced at Bill a couple of times. He was talking to Matthew and a couple of other men she did not know. He made his way to her just as she had finished taking the last photo and congratulated the family being honored that evening.

On the way out of the building, Bill said, " It's folks like you met tonight—that's why I like small towns."

"I'm beginning to see the advantages," she said.

Her climb into Truck was a repeat, as ladylike as possible, but this time she felt a hand on each side of her waist. She calmed the flutters with a simple, "Thank you."

"You're quite welcome," he said, and she noticed he did not hurry away this time. As a matter of fact, his walk to the driver's side was slow and steady.

"This has been a nice evening," she said when he got seated.

"Your company has made the difference. Barbara's right. It's been a while since I took a lady out for the evening." His gaze was steady and filled with purpose. "I was only half kidding when I said I was funning her about changing this solo routine. Caron, I'd like to see more of you. What'cha think?"

Even though the pickup cab was dim, business signs on the front of buildings provided enough light to reflect on his face, and the slight upturn of his mouth.

"I'd like that," she said.

The ride back to her apartment was not long enough. It was only nine o'clock. She didn't want to see the evening end, and when he pulled Truck into the parking spot beside her car, she asked if he wanted to come in for coffee or a glass of wine.

"I'll have what you're having. Wait and I'll get the door. That's quite a step down in those heels."

She did wait, and watched in the mirror as he started to her side of the vehicle. She observed his hesitation then fast steps to reach her door. He took her hand and she swung her legs to the edge of the seat and this time placed both feet on the side board.

When she had both feet on the pavement, he said, "Stay right here. I want to check something," and released her hand. He walked around to her vehicle. She watched as he put a hand on the back fender and leaned over.

"What's wrong?" she said.

"Thought I was seeing things when we pulled into the parking lot. There's two flat tires on your car."

"What?" She stepped around the back of Truck to get a better view of the tires. "No way. I don't believe this."

A couple of quick steps and he was on the other side of the car. She heard low mutters but could not make out what he was saying. His next words sent a spiral of hot flashes down her spine.

"These are flat, too."

She hurried to the other side to see for herself. "No."

"I've seen my share of one, maybe two, but never four

flats." He sort of laughed and shook his head at the same time. "Where did you go today, a nail factory?"

All she could do was stare at the tires. "I haven't been any place other than routine calls—mostly stayed in the office."

"There's not a lot I can do tonight. I'll come back in the morning and take care of it."

"Well, come on in for at least a glass of wine before you go. Four flats? What are the chances of that happening?"

She rummaged in her purse to get the key at they went into the foyer. He took the key and unlocked the door. Inside, the phone was ringing. He moved to allow her room to pass.

"Let me catch this." She dropped her purse and camera satchel on the sofa and hurried to answer the phone.

"Hello."

"You got four flat tires?"

She cringed to hear the familiar voice and laugh that seared her ear. Her hand was forced against the wall for support. The stalker—no question about it. He had found her.

CHAPTER 11

"You looked good enough to eat in that silky white blouse you wore tonight." Smacking, tongue clicking noises, and a string of "yum yums," turned Caron's knees to jelly She fought to keep from emptying the contents of her stomach right there on the living room floor. A deafening disconnect and dial tone grew until it was a roar in her head.

The words that forced their way between her lips were no louder than a whispered hiss. "He's here. He found me."

Her mouth became dry as the bolls of cotton she had seen being harvested earlier that week. She could not breathe. The hand that held the receiver shook.

Bill had moved closer. Her body, a mass of quivers, leaned into him. She craved his nearness and pushed back to feel him against her as if by doing so she would absorb his strength.

"What's wrong?" His voice, low and steady, emphasized each word. "Who's he and what do you mean, 'he found me'?"

Her body sagged, and his arms encircled her waist. "You need to sit down and tell me what's going on." He guided her to the sofa, but would not release his hold until she was settled against the cushioning, then sat as near as he could and still observe her face.

It was not a story she could keep to herself any longer. The moisture in her eyes thickened and tears slid down each cheek. She became totally lost in his arms when he pulled her against his broad chest.

"He's a stalker—was after me when I lived in Los Angeles. I had to move." Her voice broke and the next words were barely audible, lost in the sounds of muffled sobs. "On the phone, he said I had flat tires."

Bill nudged her away, but only enough to wipe her wet cheeks with his thumbs. "You need to tell me all about it."

She scooted away from him but not out of reach. His hold on her hands was firm and reassuring as she began the story, starting with the incidental collision into the stranger at the deli.

"Had you ever seen him before?"

"Never. I went back to work and forgot all about it. The newspaper building is next door to the deli. I got the first call that evening." The rest of the story tumbled into a succession of chronicled incidents—phone calls, notes, and threats against her friend Bruce.

"Was this your boyfriend?"

"No, Bruce is my friend. We worked together but had our own social lives. He even stayed overnight when my apartment was broken into."

She felt something akin to relief when she saw the sparks in Bill's eyes change to darts. His lips pulled into thin lines and creases on his forehead became so connected his eyebrows were almost a single line above his eyes.

His voice changed from low and steady to more authoritative. "What did the police say?"

"I couldn't definitely identify the man. We knew it was

the one I ran into at the deli. But it happened so fast there was not a full description. He mentioned things only he would know. They said they'd try to help but couldn't promise anything."

"What about the apartment break-in?"

"They made a report, but nothing ever came of it. They increased patrols around the complex."

"Telephone numbers couldn't be traced?"

"We turned what numbers we had over to the investigating officer."

"What did he say?"

Bill did not stop his barrage of questions, one after the other, but they were not fired at her in a quick succession of hard lines like investigation scenes she had seen on TV crime shows. They were direct and in a calm tone.

"The calls were made from public places, a service station, gym, restaurant—always some place different. They talked to employees but so many people were in and out of the buildings they didn't hear or see anything unusual."

"What was the time frame when it started and then your move to North Fork?" His questions continued steady as a rock.

"Almost a year. Bruce had a fraternity buddy whose father owned the newspaper here."

"This Bruce is a real important person in your life?" She felt his body tense.

"Bruce is the type of friend I could call on anytime for anything. There was no relationship other than being buddies."

"You've become an obsession to this stalker."

"What?"

"Stalkers. They become obsessed with their victim. Sometimes all it takes is the slightest look, even an unintentional smile."

"I thought I was safe. Bruce was worried. We stay in contact. He called to let me know someone broke into his apartment. Nothing was missing, but he said papers on his desk where he also kept my letters were scattered. The stalker must have found my new telephone numbers. I gave them to Bruce in a letter. I hadn't changed to a new cell phone service yet, or he would have that number. There have been a couple of uncomfortable moments over the last few weeks but I blamed it on the aftereffects of everything that happened in California—then this tonight. He even knew what I was wearing."

"Is this the reason you don't use your real name?"

"That's the primary reason, but it's still not unusual for writers to use pseudonyms."

"I think you could use that glass of wine now," he said.

While she poured two glasses, he removed his jacket and put it across the easy chair. As she sat down near him, the reality of her situation hit hard. She took a big gulp of wine as the thought crossed her mind. Bill would be driving back to the farm and she would be alone. This time it was the fear that made the moisture in her eyes turn into fresh tears.

He reached across the narrow space between them and his hand caressed the back of her neck, threaded strands of her hair between his fingers. He took her wine glass and set it on the end table along with his and brushed her wet cheeks with his palm.

"You might as well go put on your pajamas. I'm here for the night. We'll discuss the rest of the weekend tomorrow. We'll get the tires fixed. I have friends in law enforcement. I'll get in contact with them."

A surge of relief must have covered her face. "Thank you. I won't have to sleep with an eye and ear open."

The corners of his mouth lifted in response. "I'll be doing that," he said, and pulled her to him so hard she grunted when the air was pushed out of her lungs. He glanced at the sofa. "This makes into a bed?"

"Yes."

"Then I'd say we're set for the night."

By the time she had finished her last sip of wine the remaining space between them was closed and her head rested against his shoulder. When she lifted a hand to stifle a yawn, he chuckled. "Why don't you go get in your nightclothes."

She lifted her head and could not prevent the half laughing sound that made it to her throat. "Token won't mind you spending the night with another woman?"

This time his laugh was even a bit lighter. "She'll get over it, I'm sure."

Her nightclothes were warm-up pants, a large T-shirt, and socks, a statement of her preference for comfort. She knew her choice was right when she walked back into the living room and the corners of his eyes crinkled in an upward movement as if he wanted to laugh.

"I like comfort," she said.

"I like the way you think," he said. "Come here."

She didn't hesitate and settled next to him on the sofa.

"Not close enough," he said.

She lifted her legs onto the cushions and pushed with her foot as he embraced her with both arms. There was a gentle pressure on top of her head. He had pressed her against his chest and she knew it was his chin or cheek from the vibration when he said, "You're safe. I'm here."

With the full glass of wine and his reassuring comfort, she relaxed and for the moment put the stalker out of her mind. She knew by the movement he had turned up the glass to finish his wine, then placed the stemware on the end table. His arms tightened around her and she scooted a little lower into the sofa. She found herself almost prone to his chest. Her desire was not to move, but she had to.

"Let's get this sofa made up. Umm. I'll get the extra blankets and a pillow. I'm so glad you're here. I feel better."

"That wine will help you sleep. I'm going to stay up a while. I want to do a little thinking. We'll talk in the morning."

"No argument from me. I'll sleep well tonight."

* * *

HE LISTENED for the faint sounds of Caron getting into bed before he removed his boots, turned off the living room light, and sat down in the recliner. His hand pushed on the leg rest lever and, when he was comfortable, he interlocked his fingers and rested them on his stomach.

As a state trooper he had no authority to initiate an investigation in this instance, but he had contacts in the law enforcement agencies. She lived in the city limits, so it may fall under police investigator's jurisdiction. He would find out. No possibility would be ignored. He would make sure of that. He would call in favors. He chucked a list of contacts into a mental file when his thoughts wandered to Caron.

An onslaught of familiar emotions had started to race around his chest when he first saw her. Now, something really warm and welcoming was melting the cold pit in his stomach.

She was so little. He could not prevent the smile that played on his lips as he reclined in her chair. He'd just put her in his pocket and carry her around with him to make sure she was safe. The smile turned into a huge grin at this physical impossibility, but it subsided and even he could feel his forehead crease.

What was it that drew him to her? All he knew was when he saw her at the accident the first inclination was to put up a wall. However, he had no control over the surge of awakened feelings when she slipped into his arms and he prevented her from falling. An assault of feelings coursed through his body so hard it rocked his senses into a state of disbelief.

When he found out she was a reporter, an immediate memory flashed through his mind—his friend Pat in West Virginia. When he'd first met her, his ladies' man charisma went into automatic overdrive. It didn't take Pat long to block his romantic tendencies, but it had been a gentle rejection. Pat introduced him to Katherine, her friend from childhood, and his heart reeled, in love at first sight. Allen was the recipient of Pat's affection. They all became best friends and weathered the dark days they would eventually face together. When Pat and Katherine's lives were threatened, Allen and Bill's strength, abilities, and determination were unified in the sole purpose to save their girls.

Then at the livestock sale his sideways glance caught Caron staring, eyes bright with curiosity, and he wanted to respond and answer any question she posed. The gold flecks in her hazel eyes were like arrows piercing his armor of indifference.

He started to slip into a peaceful stupor right in the recliner, but a soft despondent cry had him up and in the bedroom in a heartbeat. A beam of light piercing a slit in the drapes fell across her face. He knelt beside the bed and pushed damp strands of hair from her forehead. The sound became a soft whimper and his heart ached when he saw the tears seep from under her closed eyelids.

"It was a bad dream," she whispered.

"Go back to sleep. I'm here with you." His fingers caressed her cheek, and he started to rise.

"Don't go."

She scooted over to make room for him. He lay down, pulled her close, and tucked her head under his chin. She sighed against his chest, the warm breath increasing his heart rhythm from a rapid pulse to pounding. He struggled to control his physical reaction, and it eased when her breathing changed to slow and even. She'd fallen back into to a deep sleep.

He did not mean for his embrace to be passionate, but reassuring. However, raw feelings that had been dormant for so long were persistent and he had to battle to control his body. Her needs were important—her safety came first.

His arm tightened around her. *I want to protect her, but I want to come in out of the cold. I've been out there too long.*

Caron turned on her side and pressed against him. He was losing the physical battle—reaching the drowning point. A soft moan drifted from her lips and her breath caressed his cheek. The life preserver he had been holding was drifting beyond his reach.

CHAPTER 12

Caron did not want to remove herself from the consoling warmth next to her. She kept her eyes closed and edged closer.

He moved and she opened her eyes. There was not one wrinkle on his forehead and his lips were pursed as if pondering what to do next. His eyes locked on hers.

"Good morning," she said. She could not drink in enough of him and yearned to reach out and rub her fingers against his overnight shadow of a beard.

"Good morning," he said.

She delighted in the sound of his mellow voice and its tinge of early-morning huskiness.

His attention settled on her mouth. He blinked twice—hard. She was a bit startled when he lowered his head, but not quick enough to hide the sudden surge of red on his face.

She still expected a lip kiss.

A kiss did follow—on her forehead. The softness of his lips did not disappoint. He slid to the side of the bed and grabbed his pants from where they had been discarded on the floor. The sound of legs jamming against cloth raked across her nerve endings. He stood erect and stiff. His back remained to her as he put on the shirt. She eased from her prone position to prop on an elbow, but remained silent.

"I'm sorry for last night. It shouldn't have happened. I should have been stronger, concerned with what you are going through. It was selfish of me," he said.

He turned and faced her. The solemn expression on his face jarred the foundation of her emotional strength.

The first hint of embarrassment started to grow. She pulled at the sheet to cover her nude body and got up. They stared at each other from opposite sides of the bed.

"You didn't see me run for the door, did you?" She walked around the foot of the bed and stood in front of him. "I could have said no. Bill, I needed last night."

"I don't want you to think I'm taking advantage of the circumstances, any vulnerability."

"I would never think that. I have no regrets about last night. Do you?"

"Last night was special. You're special."

"Then, we can savor the moment, put it behind us for the time being and see what the future has in store. No regrets. Okay?"

She saw the strain in his shoulders ooze away. "No regrets, but I promise it won't happen again."

Although she begrudged his promise, she admitted silently it was the right decision at that time in their relationship.

"I'll get dressed and brew a pot of coffee," she said.

"Jack in the car?" he asked when she walked into the living room.

"It's in the trunk with the spare."

By the time coffee was brewed he was back in the apartment. She had dressed and had a full cup of coffee waiting for him when he walked into the kitchen.

"Where can I wash my hands?"

"Use the kitchen sink. There's soap in the dispenser."

He turned on the water and lathered his hands. She got another cup from the cabinet and poured her morning caffeine.

"I'll get this to Griffen's, but coffee first," he said. "Need to call Matt and tell him we'll run late. It may be around one o'clock before we can get out to his place. He'll understand when I tell him about the tires."

He took the coffee she handed him and stood very still to allow the pleasant shiver to run an unhindered course from her toes to the tips of her fingers. She made another silent confession. It was satisfying to see *this* man standing in her kitchen and drinking coffee. Watching him lean back against the sink cabinet and cross one booted ankle over the other moved her to a wistful sigh. It was loud enough for him to hear and the cup he had lifted to take another sip stopped midway to his mouth. A devilish look flashed in his eyes as an understanding of the moment passed between them.

"I want you to pack a few things to spend the weekend at my farm. You won't have to worry about anything. I've got friends I need to contact. We'll also talk about next week."

The relief she felt must have reflected in her face.

"On the way out, we'll stop off at Matt's."

Any protesting thought of doubt was dismissed in a flash. "I'll pack. How about Sunday morning? I go to the nine o'clock church service. Will you go with me?"

"I'm not real big on going to church," he said, and his expression changed to uncertainty.

"I understand."

"But under the circumstances, I'll take you. I better get one of the tires to Griffen's." He drained the last of the coffee. "Secure the door when I leave. I'll wait in the foyer until I hear you set the lock."

She did as she was told and listened to his footsteps grow fainter, followed by the apartment entrance door opening and closing and Truck's motor. The stress she had carried for months lessened with each step to the recliner where she wanted to sit and finish her coffee. Even the quiet that surrounded her was an embrace of contentment and she indulged in the luxury of understanding she could rely on Bill. It was the most she had relaxed since leaving California and wonderful. He was back much sooner than she expected.

She listened for his tap. "It's me, Caron."

When she opened the door there was one big smile on his face. "We're in luck. No repair necessary—air was let out of your tires. They loaned me an air pump. All I need to do is plug it in the car outlet. It'll have the tires inflated in no time. We'll drop it back by Griffen's when we start for the farm. Packed?"

"Not yet. I wasn't expecting you back *this* soon. I'll do it right now."

She hurried to the bedroom and he went outside to air up the tires. By the time the humming sound of the air pump motor stopped, she was packed and ready to go.

She waited in her car when they got back to the tire store and he took the pump inside. He spoke briefly to one of the employees and shook hands with him, then walked back to her car. The window was rolled all the way down by the time he reached her side of the vehicle.

"Just thanking David for the use of the pump—wouldn't charge me a penny. Ready to go?"

"I'm ready. Bill, this means a lot to me—everything you're doing."

"You're going to be safe. I'll see to that." He reached into the window. His fingers touched her cheek and he slid a thumb back and forth across her chin. The care in that simple gesture filled her with such an overwhelming emotion her eyes grew moist.

"Let's go to Matt's," she said.

As she followed him out of town her heart swelled with a new confidence and it started with the blessing of meeting Bill. He knew her story and the horrific experience. She no longer had to fence and dance around the truth. For a brief moment she took her eyes off the road and lifted them to the sky to say "thank you." He had also experienced a life-changing trauma and she wanted to be his comforter.

Two children, somewhere around eleven or twelve years old, were sitting in swings hanging from the limb of a huge oak when they pulled into the driveway. They sat very still and watched as she and Bill got out of their vehicles. Matt came out of the front door, followed by Molly. The kids moved to stand by their parents.

"Four flat tires. That's the pits," Matt said as he made quick steps to Bill. "What do you think happened?"

"Somebody probably thought it would be funny—glad it was only the air." Bill's explanation was accepted without further questions. He glanced at Caron with a half smile.

"Hey, Molly. Hm. You're cooking apples," Bill said

Caron was thinking what Bill said out loud. The aroma created images of apple pies with flaky golden crusts hot from the oven.

"Molly, this is Caron Kimble. And these two—Brandon and Alex. Hey, kiddos. Ya'll helping Mama cook apples?"

"They're taking a little break. They've been a big help with the peeling. Everyone works on the farm," Molly said. "Caron, it's good to see you again and finally meet you, even though I put a big question mark on the company you're keeping." She glanced at Bill and the twinkle in her eyes turned into a full ripple of laughter as she moved to put her arms around his waist in a welcoming hug.

"I want to know, Matt, how did you end up with a jewel like Molly? Molly, divorce him and run away with me," Bill said.

Caron had a pinprick of jealousy for their obvious friendship.

"No way. Molly gets enough punishment putting up with me. With you it'll be going from bad to worse," Matt said, jumping into the word foray.

Molly hooked her arm through Caron's and nudged her along to the front door. "Come on, Caron. Let's leave these two to go look at that calf. I need to stir the apples. Brandon, Alex—break's over—back to peeling. And, Matt, I need more apples when ya'll get finished. You might just as well bring in another box of jars, too."

Caron decided she was going to like Molly.

A heavy aroma tickled Caron's nostrils as they stepped inside the house and she inhaled deeply. Her lungs filled with the bouquet, a reminder of her mom's kitchen during apple season. Brandon and Alex traipsed behind them as they all continued to a back room of the house.

There was almost a collision of bodies when Molly turned and gave the kids directions.

"This is my work room. Matthew added it a few years ago. It leaves the kitchen free to prepare meals." Two dishpans of apples bubbled on one stove and next to it a smaller heater that held a canister of quart jars. The room was overly warm even with the windows open. "These need to cook a bit longer, but I'm going to steal a small pot full. Alex, keep them stirred and turn off the stove in about thirty minutes."

"Okay, Mama." Alex settled in a chair beside Brandon and picked an apple from the half emptied basket.

"Caron, we'll make some fried pies?"

Her emotional high upon arriving at the farm dropped several notches. She became embarrassed. "Molly, I have a confession. I don't know a lot about baking. When Mama baked, she opted to be alone in the kitchen—didn't want me or Dad underfoot and in her way."

"Are you an only child?" Molly asked.

"Yes."

"I love having family and visitors in my kitchen. It's the center of our family's social time—where we share and catch up on events each day. Come on, you can watch."

"And learn," Caron said.

Her respect for Molly rose another level as she watched her agile movements, opening cabinets and pulling together the ingredients to make and briefly knead the dough. Portions were pinched off and the thuds of a rolling pin in action filled the room.

"Those men will want coffee with these pies," Molly said.

"Now I can handle that," Caron said.

"The coffee's up there," Molly said and pointed floured fingers to a cabinet. "The coffee maker is over there on the counter."

Molly spooned apples in the centers of almost wafer-thin dough and pressed little scallops around the edges with her thumb. She then brushed the edges with a light coating of egg white. As she gingerly placed each pie into the huge iron skillet, Caron watched in admiration as the hot oil bubbled and turned the pies golden brown.

"I'm afraid my lack of knowledge in the kitchen is showing," Caron said. "You make it look so easy."

Molly's laughter erupted as she lifted one of the pies from the skillet with a spatula and transferred it to a huge platter.

"I've been cooking most of my life. Mom never quite recovered after my youngest brother was born. I was the eldest of seven. It became my responsibility to help with the cooking and housekeeping." She stopped and looked at Caron. "Where did you and Bill meet?" The inquiry was asked in a tone that wasn't nosy, but as part of a chatty conversation.

Caron kept her smile inside for how many people could say, "It was at a car accident. I was taking pictures—almost fell and he caught me."

"Oh, how romantic." Molly's eyes closed and her entire face became a blossom of light. "Not the accident, but how you met"

Caron detected a tad of wistfulness in her voice when she said, "Your job sounds exciting."

"I don't know about exciting. It has its ups and downs like any other job."

"All I've ever known is farm life—up with the chickens every morning, seven days a week. Oh, don't get me wrong. I love this life, and the children are my joy. Meeting Matthew was the best thing that ever happened to me. Seems like we were made for each other—him a third-generation producer, me being raised on a farm, but ours was a lot smaller."

"How long have you known Bill?" Caron asked.

"Almost since he moved here. Matthew and Bill started doing business together and became good friends." She added more pies to the skillet and paused, her hand holding the spatula above the frying pastries. "He wasn't married but a year before he lost his wife—oh, I'm probably talking out of turn."

"She was killed in a car accident Barbara Graves said."

"Oh, you know Barbara."

"One of the first persons I met after getting settled. She became a first friend."

"Well, you couldn't have found a better one. She's knows everyone—been at the extension office for years."

Molly lifted another pie out of the skillet, hesitated, and looked directly at Caron. "I don't get to see Bill as often as

Matthew, but I've never seen him look happier. I could see a difference in him at the Farm City Banquet."

"We get along really well. What was he like before?" Caron could not prevent this question from slipping in the conversation. She wanted to know more about his past, too.

"Oh, my goodness. He was like a walking dead man when I first met him, no smile—not a sour puss, mind you, but such sad eyes."

Caron wanted to know more, but they were interrupted by the sounds of Bill and Matthew's voices and the front door closing.

"Where are the cups?"

"In that cabinet," Molly said. "Sugar substitute, too, if you use it, and cream is in the refrigerator."

Before Caron could get the cups, Bill and Matthew were in the kitchen. They came to a quick stop, eyes searching and finding the platter stacked with pies. Matthew sidled up to Molly, put his arms around her waist, and nuzzled the back of her neck.

"Matthew Harrison, you stand back and stop that. If ya'll want pies and coffee you better get out of the way and sit down. We'll bring it to the table. Now git." She pushed her buttocks backward to shove Matthew away.

Caron ducked her head to hide the laugh. Molly's orders were fierce, but Caron heard the happy lilt in her voice.

"Guess we better do as she says, Bill. That woman is the boss around here."

"And don't you forget it," Molly said, and made a threatening wave of the spatula at him as she spoke.

"Brandon, Alex, pies are ready. Come set the table." They hurried into the kitchen, got dessert plates and glasses from the cabinet, and milk from the refrigerator. Molly placed the pies in the center of the table and Caron poured the coffee.

When they were all seated, Matt said, "Brandon."

Caron watched and followed suit when heads bowed.

"Dear Lord, we thank you for the apple pies Mama made. Amen."

Matthew lifted the platter and started passing it to his right. "Bill, you're going to have Thanksgiving dinner with us, right? And, Caron, you, too."

Molly echoed the invitation. "Oh, yes, please. There's always enough food to feed an army. How about it?"

"You can count on me," Bill said. "I'm on days that week." He turned to Caron as his fork lifted a pie from the platter and put it on his plate. "How about it?"

"I would love it. Thanksgiving week is a favorite time for me. I was always so fortunate to get home for the holiday, but won't get there this year."

"Where's home?" Molly asked.

"Seattle, Washington. I haven't been at the newspaper long enough to get three or four days off for the travel time it would take to get home. It'll be a busy week, however. Our church will be helping with the community dinner this year. I volunteered to wash and bag turkeys."

"That's a big job. Not by yourself, I hope," Matthew said.

"Just part of a team. We're only going to be responsible for preparing forty of them. Another church will do the other forty."

"If you kids are through eating, go finish that basket of apples. That will be the last cooking for today. It won't take long to get them canned."

Caron was impressed with how well Brandon and Alex respected their mother's directions without complaining and even put their plates in the dishwasher.

"We have to get on to the farm," Bill said. "Token will think I deserted her."

"Give me a second. I want to wrap some pies for ya'll to take with you," Molly said.

111

Bill was quick in his reply. "No complaints from me. This has been a real treat."

"Now, remember, plan on Thanksgiving dinner here," she said, handing the pies to Caron. "Come on out early, Caron. There'll be folks in and out all day. Bill, get here when you can."

"Count on it. Thanks for the pies, Molly. Ready to head to the farm, Caron?"

"I'm ready." She did not miss an understanding look that passed between Matthew and Molly.

CHAPTER 13

Token could not stop performing a happy dance, leaping and jumping the minute she saw them pull into the driveway. When Bill got out of Truck, two paws landed against his chest and excited wails disrupted the peaceful countryside. "Hey, pretty girl. Did you think I wasn't coming home?"

"It's my fault, Token." Those words brought the excited Border Collie to her side. "Your master is home. Am I forgiven? Is everything all right now?" A hand lick and thigh nudge was her answer.

They walked side-by-side into the house, Token hot on their heels. "This has been a fantastic afternoon," she said.

"You got that right. Come on, I'll show you where you're bunking." Bill led the way and she followed.

"Matthew and Molly are such nice people. Now, Bill, I'm staking claim to one of those apple pies. Molly is a great cook. Uh—cooking has never been my strong suit. I can just imagine what Thanksgiving at their house is going to be like."

Bill said nothing and she couldn't tell by the expression

on his face and spread of his lips whether he was laughing at her confession of lacking culinary talent or happy she liked his friends.

"You get first choice of the pies," he said.

Caron dropped her overnight case and purse on the bed.

"When you get settled, I'll be in the living room. I've got calls to make," he said.

As she put her makeup pouch on the dresser and clothes in the closet, any uncertain jitters she may have had about the decision to spend a weekend at the farm faded and were replaced by a secure feeling. She locked away their shared intimacy in a secret compartment of cherished memories in her heart. Then she focused on a study of the room.

It wasn't fancy. Windows lacked drapes but were covered with Venetian blinds. The head of a standard-sized bed, with a plain comforter, took up space against one wall. Anyone entering the room would see the foot of the bed first. The dresser and chest of drawers were the only other furniture in the room. Oval, braided area rugs covered portions of the hardwood flooring. The absence of accessories and do-dads suggested to her it was a house without a woman's touch.

She caught a few words at the end of his conversation when she returned to the living room. The tone in his voice was different from anything she had heard since their first meeting. It was low, almost guttural, each word well defined: "we'll take him out of the picture." He hung up the receiver when she reached his side.

"That didn't take as long as I thought—talked with a friend, an investigator at the North Fork Police Department. We're to meet him Monday after my shift ends. When do you get off?"

"Five o'clock under normal circumstances."

"Can you be at the police department at five-thirty?"

"I'll make it a point to be there."

"I gave Wallace some of the info. It falls under the city's jurisdiction, but he also has contacts with the sheriff's department. So both departments will have the data. We'll get this punk out of your life. What he's doing is criminal. Stalking is a crime and he's made direct threats against you."

She sat down beside him on the sofa and exhaled a deep, resigned breath. "I gave up friends, a good job, and moved because of his threats. Bruce and even law enforcement agreed I was in danger but there was nothing they could do without an accurate description of the pervert. He's followed me. He's here. I know it. Bill, I'm so tired of having to look over my shoulder."

"That's going to stop. I want you to stay here for a few days, at least until we can meet with Wallace and get something going."

"I've got a job."

"I'll follow you in to work—stay here until we figure out a course of action. You'll be safe." He paused and waited for her to respond.

It was happening again. The stalker was controlling her life. She was having to plan her day around his existence.

Bill's offer was unexpected. A weekend at his farm was one thing, but several days was another matter. She made an honest evaluation of her circumstances and considered the options.

"Okay, but let's talk about it again after we meet with your friend. I want to call Bruce and let him know what's going on."

"I'll leave you to some privacy—make a pot of coffee." He started to get up, but she put out a hand and pressed against his arm.

"Don't go. I'd like you to meet my friend, even if it is over the telephone."

She scrolled down the contact names on her cell phone

and hit the call button. One...two...three...four rings. *Maybe he's got his phone turned off.* When she thought it would go to voice mail and she'd leave a message, she heard a raspy voice.

"Bruce."

"Caron? Yeah, Caron." Bruce's voice perked up. "I was nappin'."

"Bruce, he's here. The stalker's here. He found me."

"Oh, hell. It was him. He had to be the one who broke into my apartment. Your letters were in a desk drawer. He found them. Caron, I'm so sorry. I never thought for one minute he'd go this far."

"You didn't know. Bruce, I have a friend. Bill Bonner. I met him when I had to go out and take pictures at an accident."

"Law enforcement?"

"Yes, he was the investigating state trooper. I'm spending the weekend at his farm."

A laugh from the other end of the line tingled her earlobe.

"Well, I was going to suggest you needed to hook up with someone, but this is too good."

As she talked to him, her hand slipped from Bill's arm and into a waiting, open hand. His fingers closed around hers and she felt his support in the light pressure.

"After the accident I saw Bill at a livestock sale and community service day. When he asked me to the Farm City Banquet, I said yes. Bruce, he was with me when the stalker called. The stalker was laughing when he said he'd found me."

"You told Bill everything?"

"Yes. You and I thought moving would solve the problem and after a while I could get back to Los Angeles. It didn't work. I'm so tired of being on guard and having this deranged person control my life. I didn't do anything to encourage his attention."

"You said you were at your friend's farm?"

"Yes."

"Is he handy? I'd like to talk to him."

"He's right here." She handed Bill her cell phone, settled back into the sofa cushions, and listened. The restrained tone in Bill's voice faded after the initial greetings. Tension released from his shoulders the further they got into the conversation, but straightened again when his words changed to firm and explicit.

"She's safe here. I'm not going to let her out of my sight." There was another pause. "I'll let you know how this progresses."

When he handed her the phone all he said was, "Nice guy. He's really concerned—mentioned he might fly out here during spring break."

Her excitement at seeing Bruce must have spilled onto her face. Bill reacted. For a moment the lines in his forehead deepened. Her fingers twitched, wanting to erase the worry wrinkles, but she held the desire at bay. "He's my friend. I wouldn't have survived emotionally if he had not been there for me. I've probably ruined his social life."

"It's good to have someone to rely on when there's trouble."

"Yes, and knowing Bruce, he's back in circulation. He's the kind of guy who has women falling at his feet. He can pick and choose as he pleases."

"What about you?"

"I told you, he's my valued friend. Nothing more."

The cloud of concern in his face faded.

"Let's make that coffee and I've got sandwich stuff in the refrigerator."

"And I'll have another pie. How many apple trees does Matthew have?"

"A whole orchard. It's a good piece from the main house.

You didn't see them but pickers were working. There's a good market for apples."

"So why don't you grow apples, too?"

"Not big enough. Matt's farm is large enough to diversify. It's been in his family for generations. He has cattle, apple orchards, raises sweet potatoes, Irish potatoes, soybeans, corn. These days a big producer has to be diversified to survive."

"So what happens if the cattle industry goes bust?" She had sat down in the breakfast nook while he moved around the kitchen and got the coffee brewing. Realizing he was doing all the work, she bounced out of the seat. "What can I do to help? I'm not really hungry, maybe half a sandwich."

"There's a package of meat and some cheese on the lower shelf, lettuce and tomatoes in the crisper. The other stuff is in the door shelf. To answer your question about the cattle industry, I'm not big enough for it to matter. I could absorb any downturn in the industry."

"I wonder if anyone on our staff has ever done a story on apple harvest in the county?"

"Not since I've been here," he said.

"Well, I might just have to check it out."

He handed her a loaf of bread, leaned against the counter, and crossed his arms over his chest. " Hope you're not planning on climbing any trees. I'm trying to keep you safe."

The possibility of her climbing an apple tree to get a story presented a comical mental picture. "It's only a thought."

"I'm sure Matt would be a big help if you want to do a story. How long did you say you've been a journalist?"

"Seems like all my life. I made up stories and started writing when I was in elementary school. Not having brothers or sisters, I had a lot of quiet time. Read a bunch, too. How long have you been in law enforcement?"

"Hadn't thought about getting into it until my brother got

in touch. I'd just finished a stint with the marines. He was sheriff in Mason Springs, West Virginia, and needed another deputy. That was ten years ago. When he retired I stayed on as chief deputy—moved here later."

She waited for him to tell her more but his voice dropped in volume and he turned away to get cups from the cabinet. The slight droop of his head did not escape her notice nor did an immediate lifting of his shoulders, back into pencil-straight posture. He knew her story but she would have to wait for him to share his.

He set the cream and sugar on the table, and paused for a moment to gaze out the window before settling his attention back on her. The sandwiches were made and she took them to the table while he got a bag of chips. Token took up the space between their feet under the table.

"She's waiting for a share. If something doesn't accidentally fall from the table, she'll sit down and roll those big brown eyes in the most pitiful, starving look."

"I can't stand that." Caron pulled a morsel from the corner of her sandwich and handed it to a waiting mouth. Her reward was a wet lick on her fingers.

"You've made a friend for life." He fed Token a bite of his sandwich and she crawled from under the table and stretched out on the floor while they finished eating. "Let's take our coffee to the living room. I'll make a fire."

Even the sofa felt more inviting as she scooted back, balancing the coffee in one hand to keep it from sloshing over the rim. While he stacked a few pieces of wood in the fireplace, her body relaxed as she studied the picture-perfect scene. The knowledge she was secure opened the possibilities of a new chapter in her life. Her eyes rested on the little girl's picture and its prominent place on the coffee table.

"Have you heard from your friends in West Virginia lately, the little girl's parents?"

"Yes. They may be coming in the spring." He sat down on the sofa, picked up his coffee, and took a deep sip from the cup. "I was thinking about putting up a Christmas tree this year in that corner. What do you think?"

"It's a perfect location—the first thing to be seen when company comes in the front door, near the fireplace—a postcard holiday setting."

"How about helping me decorate it?" His face screwed up in a frown, but he lifted his arm and stretched it across the back of the sofa in her direction. "I haven't put up a tree since I moved out here. It's time I did."

"I'll be glad to help. I love all the holiday decorations. I volunteered to help put them up at the church. Have we got time for a little walk before it gets too dark?"

"If we go now."

They left their cups on the coffee table. Token was right behind them when they went outside.

"This is the biggest porch I've ever seen."

"I thought so, too. It's a pretty old farmhouse. Barbara called it a wrap-around porch—a center for summertime family activities and where visitors used to sit and talk before house fans."

Their direction took them away from the house and across the yard to the fence. Caron stopped to watch the last rays of sunlight make their exit and tilted her head to listen. The countryside began to settle in its waning moments before dark. The lonely sound of a whippoorwill called in the distance. She relished the calm cloak of serenity that spread a message of quiet peace.

"This is my favorite time of the day," she said, propping her arms on the top fence plank and looking across the open field. Her eyes welled at the beauty of the sunset. "I would spend every evening right here." The fear she managed for months and the satisfying experience of that day struck an overwhelming emotional chord and unexpected moisture threatened to spill onto her cheeks. She tried to wipe it away before Bill noticed. She was not subtle enough.

His arm went around her shoulder and a gentle pull nestled her head against his chest. "It's going to be all right." She welcomed the comforting cheek pressing against the top of her head. "Come on, let's get you inside."

"Yes, let's get inside. I want to straighten up the kitchen, and get a shower. It's been a full day."

It only took a few minutes to get the kitchen in order.

"I'm going to read for a while. I got the new cattlemen's magazine this week."

"Well, I'm going to take a shower. So I'll see you in the morning," she said.

By the time her hair was dried and she put on nightclothes—a pair of warm-up pants and sweatshirt—the light in the bedroom had to be turned on. Dark claimed the countryside. It would be an early bedtime but the comfort of knowing Bill was in the living room was welcomed. She was even anxious to lie down, snuggle into the comforter, and allow herself to venture into a state of restful sleep.

The peace was welcomed, but just as she allowed its relief to deepen, a noisy squeak jarred her sweet drowsiness. It took a moment to determine its source, but the crack of seeping light left no doubt the sound came from the door to her bedroom. Caron shut her eyes in disbelief, squeezed them so tight her face hurt. He promised. *What am I going to do?*

Her eyes remained closed. The noise stopped and the silence became deafening. Weight made the side of the bed sag. Her heart pounded. She wasn't sure whether the power of awareness surging through her body was anticipation or doubt.

A soppy cheek lick, tongue against skin, answered the

question. She opened her eyes and could not stop the giggle. That resulted in a solid thumping and a length of fur stretched out against her body. Token's tail continued tapping.

"Token, if you're going to sleep in my bed you have to be still." Caron recognized the deep sigh as a state of contentment when her hand rested on the Border Collie's head.

CHAPTER 14

A skirmish was underway in Caron's drowsy state of mind—the desire to remain cuddled under the comforter versus getting up and follow the aroma of bacon cooking.

It's so early. She could not resist and gave the ball of silky fur beside her a nudge. "Hey." Token stretched and issued a soft, deep-throated cry and slapped a paw on Caron's cheek. "Well, come on. I need to go, too."

Token jumped off the bed. Caron's legs dangled from the side for a couple of seconds. She wiggled her toes a good morning before both feet landed on the rug and she hurried toward the bathroom. Token scampered in the opposite direction. A muffled voice from the kitchen, the opening and closing of a door, confirmed her assessment Token needed to get outside.

She splashed cold water on her face and did a quick run through her hair with a brush. It would have to do. A need that could only be filled with the first cup of coffee directed her steps to the kitchen.

"Good morning." The sound was so husky and melodious the need for caffeine was shoved on hold and her progress halted so fast it made the skin on the bottom of her feet tingle. Nothing could have prepared her for what stood waiting in the kitchen.

Her eyes filled with the image of a man at complete ease, leaning against the counter connected to the stove. Bill held a long fork in one hand and a cup of coffee in the other. She licked her lips to make sure drool wasn't sliding from the corners of her mouth. It was the most sensuous site she had ever seen, from the bare feet to a sleeveless T-shirt, its material stretching only to his midsection and hip-hugging sweat pants.

When he shifted his focus to turn strips of the frying bacon, she was privy to a side view of a flat stomach. The only sound in the room was sizzle and the occasional pop of hot grease from the skillet.

His attention returned to her. What she saw in his face changed her insides to molten lava, but the smoky haze faded when she locked on and returned the stare. Any emotion he had was checked and his expression became unreadable.

"Cup's on the table. Breakfast will be ready in five minutes. Have a seat."

Her struggle to calm butterflies diving against the insides of her tummy and make sure she gave a coherent answer was successful. "This is a treat. I usually grab a honey bun and stop by the deli for coffee."

He brought the coffee pot to the table and poured her a full cup. Caron reacted to the first breath of air swirling from his movement and inhaled, filling her lungs with a soapy clean aroma.

"You wanted to attend early church service. I thought I'd cook a weekend breakfast."

"Token paid me a visit last night and stayed."

He turned aside but not fast enough before she heard a low mutter, "Lucky dog."

Caron's coffee sloshed from the cup when her hand twitched in reaction to those words. Her full attention stayed on the tabletop to keep the giggle at bay.

"I dozed after reading a while—couldn't find her when I woke. I saw the door ajar and figured she was probably with you. I did a quick peek to make sure. You were both sound asleep."

"She's a real fur baby. I could not have a pet in Los Angeles. Most apartment complexes would not allow them. Token's special."

"That she is," Bill said.

"I appreciate everything you're doing, Bill, but really if you don't want to go to church I'll be fine."

He took a sip of his coffee. "I'd feel better going and not sitting around here wondering."

He dished bacon onto a platter and filled the skillet with a bowl of whisked eggs before lifting a pan of biscuits from the oven. A split saucer of jam and butter had already been placed on the table. *Hm, a man who can cook, and be my protector too? What more could a woman want on a Sunday morning in November?*

"Oh. I can't forget Wednesday. Got to be at the church—turkeys to wash and bag."

"What time? And, by the way, your presence here is my pleasure."

"We meet at five o'clock in the fellowship hall kitchen on the south side of the church."

"My shift ends at four. I'll come by."

She missed the sensuality in the voice that greeted her earlier but appreciated the reassuring tone in his words.

"It makes me mad that this man is controlling my life. I get angry every time I think about it."

Bill moved the platter, now full of bacon, eggs, and biscuits, to the table and slid onto the seat across from her.

"I think we'll get something going after our meeting with Wallace tomorrow afternoon. He's the best, moved here from New York City. He worked there in police investigations." A knowing smile spread across his mouth. "He got tired of big city life, too."

"I'll admit my stress level is dropping." She scooped a serving of eggs from the platter, added a couple slices of crisp bacon, and reached for a biscuit. All she wanted at that moment was to enjoy breakfast with the man who sat across the table drinking his coffee.

Token scratched at the door. Bill got up to let her inside. She took up her place under the table. Thoughts of the stalker were erased and that Sunday morning the simple joy of having a weekend breakfast took precedence.

They couldn't linger over coffee.

"We should leave here by 7:30," Caron said.

"I'll be waiting in the living room. We'll clean the table when we get back." She saw even white teeth when he paused and gave her a big smile. "It wouldn't be the first time I've left dishes on the table and go on to work."

He *was* standing and waiting by the time she had put on makeup and dressed.

"Token, you want to stay in or go out? We won't be gone all day." Her excited leap to the door was his answer.

"Caron, we'll go in my SUV. Pull yours to the side of the house so it won't be visible from the road. Just want to take precautions."

Images chilled the November sun and skewered her pleasant Sunday morning thoughts as she walked to the car.

Anger smoldered as she thought of the stalker who was controlling her life.

Their conversation was limited on the way into North Fork. Caron wondered why Bill did not attend church but wasn't about to ask since those preferences were entirely personal.

"After church, let's stop by the apartment. I want to check inside. Make sure everything is okay."

"We'll sure do that," he said.

She was aware of observant eyes from members of the congregation after ushers handed them church bulletins and they proceeded down the middle aisle. A couple of empty spaces on a pew caught her attention. With their addition to the row of worshipers, by the time they settled his hip was a solid mass of rock against hers.

A church bell tolled to begin the service and the congregation stood for the opening hymn followed by a prayer. As the words flowed from the pulpit, Caron felt the muscles tense in the arm that touched hers. Bill's eyes were aligned to the front of the church. She wanted to place a reassuring hand on his arm, but that might be mistaken as patronizing, so she remained still.

Reverend Jon began to talk about the pain and turmoil a person may face at some point in their life and its solution came from the heavenly source of love. Seated for the closing prayer, she felt tension lessen in the hip that had remained against hers the entire service. She did a sneak peek and Bill's head was bowed lower than the other worshipers around them. His hands were clasped so tight the knuckles paled.

At the end of the service they stood for the benediction. Reverend Jon reminded the congregation about the church decorations. Caron and Bill sidled into the aisle with other members of the congregation to leave. It was only a few blocks to the apartment complex. Bill drove without saying a word. The silence continued even when they pulled into the parking lot.

"I'll be right back. This won't take but a jiffy." Caron hurried into the apartment foyer, unlocked the door, and did a quick walk-through.

"Everything alright?" he asked, when she returned.

"It's just fine," she said. "I knew it would be, but wanted to check."

They were at the city limits before he spoke again. "That sermon hit home." The words were soft, the tone almost reverent.

"I believe we've all had our share of pain. For some the hurt lasts longer," she said.

The silence in the SUV was not uncomfortable. She had her own thoughts and assumed he had his, so was surprised when he pulled to the side of the highway.

Bill turned to her. "I'm sorry. Don't know where my mind is. Let's go back to town. I'll take you out to lunch."

"That's not necessary."

He stared out the front windshield into space, then back to her. "I have barbecue in the freezer—buns, chips...pickles."

"That's fine with me."

He pulled back on the highway. A satisfying ambience settled in the vehicle until they stopped in the driveway. Token changed all that when she jumped off the porch and ran to meet them.

She could hear Bill say, "Yeah, that's my pretty girl," as she got out of the SUV and walked around to be with them and give Token a scratch-massage on the back.

"You are a pretty girl. I've never had a fur baby. Will you be my buddy, too?" Token's head coming up from the back rub to push against Caron's hand, plus a quick lick on her extended fingers, was the answer. "I'm glad she likes me."

"What's not to like? She and I have a mutual interest." Token followed them inside.

Caron allowed his words to slide over her like a serving of warm honey.

"Come on. Let's thaw out the meat and we'll make sandwiches." He removed the sports jacket and continued in the direction of the kitchen.

Caron cleared the table and put the dishes in the dishwasher while Bill thawed the meat and laid out buns and chips on the counter. "Do you want pickles?"

"Absolutely," she said and wet a dishcloth to wipe the table. "What do you normally do on Sunday afternoon?"

He shoved his hands into oven mitts and took a plate of steaming meat out of the microwave. "Token and I keep the sofa occupied. Sometimes we'll go out and ride around the place. What do you do?"

"I usually don't leave the apartment. I go by the diner after church for lunch and I'm at home for the rest of the afternoon. Hm, that meat smells good."

"I have a friend who is in the catering business and he's the best when it comes to smoking meats." He added buns and chips to the table beside the meat and went back for the pickles.

"I'm glad we didn't eat lunch in town," she said. "I'd much rather be sitting right here."

He speared barbeque from a platter with a fork and piled it on a bun. His next sentence caused chill bumps to break out on her arms and run amok across her shoulders. Her attention riveted to his face.

"Caron, I'll make a confession. I knew you were special the first time I literally ran into you. When the time is right, I want this relationship to be long-term." He stopped, looked up from the sandwich he was making, folded his arms and rested them on the table. He waited for her response.

Although she was a bit jolted by his direct statement, she had no qualms about the answer. "I'd like that, too." The heat on her insides erupted in a bright blossom all the way to her hairline. He must have understood the blush for he smiled and then chuckled.

"Good and we'll get this bastard off your back so you can have a normal life."

It was the best barbeque sandwich she had ever eaten, and admitted it wasn't the meat, sauce, or chips, but Bill's presence on the opposite side of the table that made it so delectable.

He gave Token a piece of meat. "Pretty girl, Caron's going to be visiting more often." With that, his expression included a wide smile. "You okay with that, Token?" It wasn't a bark that came from under the table—more like a subdued woof. "See, Token knows a good thing when she meets it, too."

"You two are a pair. I'll take you both."

After the table was cleared Bill started the dishwasher. They carried their refills of tea into the living room and sat on the sofa.

"After that meal I think I'm going to need a nap. Bill, thanks for going to church with me."

He stretched an arm across the top of the sofa. When he spoke his voice echoed quiet reassurance. "It's been a long time since I attended church services. It was a good feeling."

He changed positions and reached to pick up the photo album from the coffee table. As he placed an elbow on each knee and held it in both hands, she could not see his facial features, but even the side view made her aware of the solemn moment.

"Most of the story is in here—in pictures." He put the book back on the coffee table but left it open. "I met Katherine when I was working as a chief deputy in West

Virginia with the Mason Springs Sheriff's Department." He did not move but kept his focus on the album.

From where Caron sat the first page was visible, a photo of Bill and a smiling bride standing close beside him. His attention refocused on Caron, and his beckoning eyes invited her to look at the album. She moved closer and waited for him to speak, understanding what was transpiring. He was sharing his pain.

"This is Katherine—Kat. The little girl in the picture was named after her. Katherine was killed in an automobile accident. We'd only been married a year. I was so angry and then depressed—asked God why she had to die." He turned to the next page.

"I'm so sorry, Bill."

"I shut out everything and everybody. It was Pat, Katherine's friend, and mine, too, who yanked my chain hard and made me face reality. I had to get on with my life. I couldn't do that in West Virginia, so ended up here. Katherine was gone. Like I told you, I had originally passed through this area on the way to West Virginia to take the deputy job—fell in love with it."

"That's why you hadn't been to church for a while."

"Exactly." He turned to another page. She sat very still and looked at each page—photo after photo of Katherine. It dawned on her. There was no jealousy of seeing pictures of another woman—Bill's wife. This was important. He was making it a point to share his past.

"It's been over three years since Katherine was killed. They said it was instant—she didn't suffer. A drunk driver hit her head on."

"Was he charged?"

"Yes. First degree manslaughter. Driving under the influence among other charges. It'll be a long time before he's back on the highways."

"I've never lost anyone close—had friends who grieved losing a family member. I saw how hard it was on them."

"It's been a while. I pretty much refused to let anyone in my life and have never invited a woman to my place."

That said, he gazed at her, stretched out both hands, and closed the book.

CHAPTER 15

Caron shifted her concentration from the highway to the rearview mirror long enough to glimpse Bill following in Truck. She relaxed and welcomed the sweet euphoria of knowing he was there. The stress she had accepted as a normal part of her life started to lift and was being substituted with an exuberance of relief. It had been a weekend of discovery. Bill had told her about Katherine. When he closed the photo album, words were not necessary.

I'm ready. It had been months—a couple of years since she had allowed herself the luxury of any relationship other than friendship with Bruce. The fear of displaying a simple courtesy to any man had filled her with emotional apprehension. Any gesture, meant to be amiable only, might result in mistaking her actions.

The next glance in the mirror, tracing the outline of Bill's image in Truck, heightened her state of relaxation. A deep satisfying sigh filled the inside of the vehicle.

Bill maneuvered Truck into the empty space next to her vehicle when she pulled into the parking lot.

He hurried to open her door. "I'll walk with you," he said, and cupped her elbow in his hand.

Caron laughed. "I was just thinking," she said. "You—the uniform. If anyone here noticed, they might question why you're escorting me into the newspaper building. It could appear as if I've done something wrong."

The corners of his eyes crinkled. "Well, I'll just have to come up with a charge and take you prisoner."

"Now, that could develop into an interesting scenario."

"Well, we'll see what I can do about that," he said, and squeezed her elbow.

He stopped at the front door and placed both hands on her shoulders. They brushed against her skin as they slid to her elbows, leaving a path of welcome heat. They stood so close her lungs filled with an intoxicating blend of cleanliness and aftershave. If it had not been for the fact they were standing at the front entrance of the building, she might have submitted to a desire to ease her arms around his neck. She remained very still and enjoyed the moment.

"I'll see you this afternoon," he said, the words so quiet in tone she almost dismissed the reason he was meeting her and where they were going. "I know you've got a job to do. I'd feel better if you remained in the office. If you have to be out, remain alert to your surroundings and make sure you avoid isolated locations. Have you talked to your boss about the problem?"

"No. Until Friday night there was no reason."

"You need to let your manager know what's going on for your own safety. We'll know more after we meet Wallace." He had not removed his hands and she felt the light pressure on her arms increase. "Now, promise you're going to be careful."

"I promise."

He hesitated, turned and made long strides back to Truck.

She could see the outline of his body through the front windshield after he got in and closed the door. He hesitated before starting the motor and exiting the parking lot.

When she got to her office, she piled purse, camera satchel, and leather-bound notebook on the desk, then made sure her "good mornings" were in a pleasant tone. Jennifer and Vicki responded with quick "heys." Jennifer followed her perky response with, "Caron, can you go with me to the extension agent's luncheon today? Vicki can't make it."

"Let me go get a cup coffee. I'll be right back."

She made the trip to the break room, filled a cup so full the hot liquid sloshed over the brim a couple of times on her way back. "Now," she said, taking the first delicious sip, "where are we going?"

"It's upstairs at the Lakeland Restaurant. I'll drive."

That meant her car could remain parked. *I'm keeping my promise, Bill.*

Caron kept her smile hidden. Jennifer was the society editor and attended many club meetings. She was loyal to the social calendar of civic events and that was cause for many invitations. Jennifer rarely failed to fill requests and had asked her on more than one occasion to go along. It enabled her to become acquainted with names around the area in a short time. Going to the luncheon would also be an opportunity to see Barbara. She was curious to find out how Barbara interpreted Bill's comment about changing their relationship status.

"Susan Fulmer is going to be their guest. Remember, she's the wife of Garland Fulmer—Farm Family of the Year winners. I thought you might want to follow up with a feature story, maybe go out to their farm for a photo and story on some of her holiday recipes. I could sure use it for the Thanksgiving issue."

"Sounds like fun. Count me in."

The morning moved along like a sleepy turtle. She did not concentrate on new projects, and kept busy cleaning up files, organizing and making lists of potential story topics. They left at eleven-thirty.

Caron barely made it through the door behind Jennifer before she was face-to-face with Barbara who had a smile so bright it made the whole room seem lighter.

"You're sitting beside me. I want to know everything about you and Bill."

"Girl, how about we get together after the luncheon. I need to talk. You got your car?"

"Yes."

"Then, I'll ask you to take me back to the office if it's not out of your way. I came with Jennifer. Can we do that? I do need to share a story with you."

"Not fair. That means I have to wait until after lunch to get answers to my questions."

Caron found Jennifer and let her know the change in plans, and reintroduced herself to Susan with a promise to call for an appointment later in the week. Barbara was by her side when the meal had concluded and Jennifer took the necessary pictures.

"Do you want to hang here?" Barbara asked.

"Let's go downstairs." Caron told Jennifer she'd be back at the office in about an hour.

They found an empty booth in the back of the dining room. "Okay. From the beginning. Are you and Bill going to be a serious item?"

"Maybe, but first I need to tell you a story."

By the time Caron got to the meeting with the investigator later that day, Barbara's expression was the color of ashes.

The next sentence was at a level so low Caron had to lean forward to hear. "Why didn't you say something sooner?"

The focus that had remained so concentrated on Caron as she had related events rose and darted around the room as if she expected the stalker to be among the lunch crowd.

"There was no reason. I thought I had left him in California—until the flat tires."

"Thank God you have Bill."

"You got that right. After we got air in the tires, we went to his farm. I was there for the weekend. And, for only you to know, I may be staying out there all week."

"That makes me feel a little better. Does that mean you may take up permanent residence in North Fork?" Barbara's face had regained a normal color and having knowledge of a secret tweaked her mouth in a satisfying smile.

"Barbara, you're my friend and will be the first to know. I'm almost afraid to commit to anything, but I'll say this, Bill would be at the head of the line when I do. I have real feelings for him."

"Did he tell you about his wife?"

"He did. I believe he's closed the book on that chapter in his life."

Barbara took her back to the office and Caron completed a backlog of paper work. She called Susan Fulmer and set up an interview appointment for Tuesday before leaving to meet Bill. He was waiting in Truck when she pulled into the parking lot adjacent to the police department.

"Did you have a good day?" he asked.

"It was quiet. I kept my promise and stayed in the office most of the day—got caught up on a logjam of filing. How about you?"

"Pretty routine," he said, falling in step beside her. He stretched an arm so his hand brushed against her neck. It stayed there until they got to the glass door with an overhead sign marked POLICE DEPARTMENT.

When they went inside a woman, sitting at a desk and

perusing a clip board, got up and shuffled to the counter. "Bill Bonner, it's been ages. How are you doing?"

"Fine, Mitzi. We need to see Wallace. He's expecting us."

"I'll let him know you're here." She returned to her desk and pressed a couple of buttons on the telephone. Caron did not miss the woman's attention giving her the once-over as she spoke into the phone receiver.

"You know where his office is. Go on back."

Bill guided Caron down a hallway and into a small office where they were greeted with, "Hey, you son of a gun."

Caron made the assumption this was Wallace since he rounded his desk to shake Bill's hand. Caron suppressed an urge to laugh as she was reminded of the cartoon characters, Mutt and Jeff—Bill, tall and broad shouldered, the investigator smaller in stature with a ruddy complexion and reddish-brown hair cropped GI style.

"Man, it's a sorry day when the only way I see you anymore is when you need my help. How you doing, dude? It's been a while." One hand continued to pump and the other clapped Bill on the shoulder.

The greeting from Bill was just as exuberant. "So, how's the number one runt of the police department?"

Caron didn't mentally agree with the word "runt," but there was a blatant difference in size. A short-sleeved shirt allowed a display of bulges in his arms as he shook Bill's hand. She would put betting money on his being a capable and wiry adversary in a confrontational matter. The twinkle in his eyes may have meant to be disarming, but again a little voice told her it was probably misleading and she would bet her bottom dollar that's what he wanted other people to see as part of his demeanor.

"Busy catching criminals" he said, turning to Caron.

"Wallace, this is Caron Kimball, newspaper name¾Caron Stallings real name."

"I've seen your name in the paper." His attention went back to Bill. "Lizzie was asking about you the other night when we sat down to supper. Wondered when we were going to see you again."

"You mean you actually got to share a meal with the family?" Bill said.

"Hey, it was a slow day. Don't remind me about all the meals I've missed with the family. Lizzie doesn't let me forget it. Let's go to the conference room." He led the way and they followed.

"How are the boys?"

"Growing like weeds," Wallace said. "Seems like Lizzie needs money every week to buy clothes. Sorry you're having this trouble, Miss Kimball. Bill told me the problem. Let's sit down and talk about it."

"It's Caron. And I appreciate you taking your time to help."

"That's why we're here. Why don't you start at the beginning and tell me when and where all this began?"

Caron bent forward in her seat and crossed her arms to rest on the conference table. Bill moved his chair closer.

As Caron related everything she could remember, Wallace frowned, scooted his chair a few inches from the table, interlocked his fingers, and allowed his hands to rest across his stomach. "Stalking is a crime in Alabama. And that's what you've got—a stalker. From what you're telling me, it has been intentional and repeated. He's followed you across the country and communicated. But have there been threats, implied or direct?"

"There's been no physical threats, only harassing words like when he broke into my apartment in Los Angeles and took a pair of my undies, and he asked how I liked the flat tires."

"How do you reckon he got your apartment telephone number?"

"It had to have been when he broke into my friend's apartment in California. Bruce said the papers on his desk had been scattered. That's where he kept my letters, but he told me nothing was missing."

"That doesn't mean he didn't get the information on your location *and* telephone number." Wallace wrote on a notepad. "First of all, change your apartment telephone number and only give it to people you trust. Caution your office. Under no circumstances are they to give it out to anyone. We'll increase patrols around your apartment."

"After the tire incident and call, I wanted Caron to stay at my place—see what plan we could put into action after we talked with you," Bill said.

"Good. I'll check out the local car rental outlets and the ones close by. He may have rented a car. He's got to get around. That is, if he didn't drive cross-country in his own vehicle." He directed his attention to Bill. "I'll be up front with you, friend. There's very little info and no description." His attention went back to Caron. "Any distinctive clothing, Caron? What about a hat? Jacket—maybe an insignia? How about footwear?"

"The only thing I remember is he wore a baseball type hat that had the initials SUCS on it Nothing else was special about it. It happened so fast. That's why the investigation in LA was on the low priority list. I guess I'll have to wait until this monster confronts me," Caron said.

Bill's arm shot out and went around her shoulders. "We're not going to allow that."

"He's right," Wallace said. "The advantage we have is that being a smaller town anything out of the ordinary gets attention. How long will you be staying at Bill's?"

"How about at least this week?" Bill said.

Carol hesitated, but not for long. "I'll have to go by the apartment and get clothes."

"And I'll go with you," Bill said.

"Good," Wallace said. "That'll give me time to do some preliminary investigation—put surveillance on the apartment, get in touch with car rentals, ask a few questions. You're in good hands with Bill."

Walking back to the car, Bill encircled an arm around her waist. "Wallace is the best. In the meantime, I'll be watching your back. You'll be safe. I don't think this idiot would try anything as long as I'm around or if you're with people. He's a coward. I'd like to see him attempt to bother you at my farm. He'll get all he can handle, and more."

Caron responded with a playful bump of her hip against his. "I'm glad you're with me."

The grip he had on her waist tightened.

CHAPTER 16

Bill retrieved Caron's luggage and waited for her at the front of Truck. She pulled the purse strap over her shoulder and paused, scanned the front seat to determine if there was anything else she needed before going in the house.

"I need to walk off this nervous energy," she said as they went inside. "Think there's enough daylight left?"

"If we hurry." Bill loosened his tie.

"It won't take me but a heartbeat to change shoes."

"I'll meet you on the front porch," he said.

The last rays of sunlight were starting to fade when they took the first step into the yard.

"Caron, I've been thinking. I'm off Wednesday. You'll have people around you at work, plus other folks at the church. While you're washing turkeys, I'll go to Matt's and get the calf, then meet you at the church to follow you to the farm."

"Sounds like a plan to me," she said. "I'm doing an interview with Susan Fulmer tomorrow. Remember, the Farm Family of the Year. The paper wants the story for the Thanksgiving edition."

"I'll be behind you on all trips into town and back. I did want you to go to Matt's with me but we can take care of everything and I can get the calf into one of the barn stalls." He bumped her shoulder in a playful gesture. "He's been weaned, but needs to get away from his mama and become familiar with his new home."

Caron stopped at the end of the barn and hesitated in front of a large stack of hay bales. She sat down, yoga style, on the one that had been pulled aside and cushioned her back against the higher stack. Bill eased down beside her, stretched his legs and crossed them at the ankles. Leaning back and propping on his elbow put Caron directly in his line of sight. He picked up a sliver of hay, put the blunt end in his mouth and held the tip between two fingers.

Token maneuvered in the space between them and pushed against Caron's thigh.

"I think she's trying to get your attention," Bill said.

Her hand automatically stroked Token's head, but she stared across the empty pasture.

"I'm tired, Bill. Irritated this man is controlling my life, frustrated I can't identify him. I'm angry. This is no way to live."

"We'll stop him." Bill shifted his weight to reach for her hand, laced his fingers in hers. "I'll be with you, and Wallace is the best. He'll track down this pervert."

The dark was closing in around them. "How about we go into the house and get a bite of supper and have a quiet evening," he said. "I need to do a little paper work that's been heckling me for attention—TV programs aren't too bad tonight."

"I think I'll read. I bought a new novel and haven't had time to get into it. A quiet evening—no worries. I like the sound of that."

Caron gave a little push with her hands and got up. Bill rose and reclaimed her hand.

He laughed and shook his head. "Just a minute," His hands began to brush sprigs of hay from the back of her sweater and removed a few broken bits before coming to rest on her shoulders. "I want to protect you."

Her gaze was drawn to the serious expression on his face, but it was the subtly quiet tone of his words she needed to hear. Caron closed the distance between them and encircled her arms around his waist. He pulled her close and tucked her head under his chin, his arms a cocoon of security. She inhaled deeply and the sigh she released broke the silence of the evening. "I believe I'm safe with you."

He pulled away. His fingers lifted her chin. She yearned for the caring look on his face to be replaced by the physical touch of his embrace. Could she dare to be so blatant? Before she changed her mind, Caron stood on tiptoe and kissed him.

His reaction was instantaneous. She was crushed against him so tight air whooshed out of her lungs. Her mouth became his target. He parted her lips and dipped his tongue inside. The taste of brown sugar cookies filled her with the promise of sweet delights.

The movement of his lips slowed and she could not prevent a little moan of protest. He did not release her, but kept her body pressed close. Her fears and anxieties were slipping into oblivion.

When he spoke, the words were firm and determined.

She descended from cloud nine and planted her feet back on solid ground.

His hands lightly squeezed her shoulders and she was gently nudged away. "When the time is right I'll make you forget all the trauma you've been through."

Bill's words cloaked her in comfort. He had made her a

promise and the commitment was reaffirmed in the strong hand that held hers as they walked back into the house.

She made it a point that evening to concentrate on the inflection of each word Bill had said, but it was thoughts of him the following morning and the interview that caused her to forget and leave the cell phone on the bedroom dresser. Its absence in her purse when she reached for it on the drive in to work, however, was dismissed as a minor infraction. She'd swing by and pick it up on the way to the Fulmer interview, but first a stop by the apartment to get her electric shaver. Her legs needed attention. Bill's last words to her that morning as he walked her to the front door of the newspaper building was a reminder to stay alert and away from isolated areas.

The morning became a battle, her mind swelling with thoughts of a relationship with Bill and the need to respond to phone messages. Images of Bill won the war and she was in a happy frame of mind when she left the office and stopped by the apartment. She was back on the road in no time and picked up speed to get to Bill's house and on to the Fulmer farm.

A panorama of fall foliage decorated the landscape and glorious colors lifted her mood to a higher level. She fingered the turn blinker on the approach to Bill's driveway and automatically looked into her rearview mirror.

The black sedan approaching from behind was traveling at a breakneck speed and she would be knocked into the next county if the driver did not alter course. A flash of foreboding made her increase speed but she had to brake and slow down to accommodate the turn into the driveway. There was not a second to spare. A cloud of dust erupted when the vehicle swerved off the side of the road to pass, horn blaring and grinding at her nerves. When she got stopped and could observe, the other vehicle was moving so fast the rear end swayed side-to-side so erratically it left rubber marks on the highway.

The seconds she sat very still to beg her breathing to return to normal turned into a minutes. *That was dangerous. Wish I could have gotten a tag number.*

* * *

PAIN. Beating his palms against the steering wheel became so excruciating it broke through Dexter's raging anger. A wail tore from his mouth and screamed his intent, "She's dead!" His right hand doubled into a fist and pounded the seat. He stretched his fingers, red from the punishment, needing to relieve the ache. "This is her fault and she's going to pay."

He pulled off the highway onto a small dirt road. His arms, board straight, locked on the steering wheel after the vehicle stopped. His mouth moved but sound was so low the idling motor drowned the words. He turned the ignition key. Quick rasping breaths became the only interruption in the silence.

Resentment churned in his stomach. It rolled and formed gushes of hatred before it spewed from his mouth. "She's no good. She's made a mockery of my love. She's gotta pay."

All the smug acknowledgements of his intelligence in finding Caron were pushed from his mind. It had been so easy to discover where she was living but following her became more difficult when that state trooper started escorting her around. He was close by the day they met for lunch. Surveillance of them was so easy as he sat in the parking lot of the shopping center across the street. He had watched as she parked and went inside. It was only a couple of minutes before the trooper arrived. Hot spears of anger slammed into his body and seeds of revenge started to build when he was subjected to the blurred images of them sitting at a booth and leaning toward each other.

Dexter was willing to forgive her at first and let the air out of her tires as a little warning. He didn't count on that trooper being there to help. She was gone from the apartment all weekend. He parked far enough away from the newspaper office on Monday and saw her with that trooper. As the probabilities increased that she had been with him all weekend, spurts of doubt festered and ached. That knowledge made him sick to his stomach, but maybe he was wrong. He would confirm his suspicions, and find out where the man lived.

The pedestal where he had placed Caron began to crack. If she had taken advantage of his emotions, led him on from the beginning, there would be consequences. He was smart and would be patient and find out where she was staying.

When she left the building, he followed. She stopped by her apartment and then headed out of town. He delighted seeing her blinker flash to turn into the driveway. That must be where she was staying, but he had to be sure.

An hour later he headed back to the house where Caron had stopped. Her car was not there. He dared to turn into the drive with the Bonner name on the mailbox. *Bonner—Bonner. That name was familiar. The lightbulb lit up in his brain. He had read it in the paper.* The furor of this discovery spilled from his mouth, the first word a delightful "gotcha" accompanied by a spreading of his lips into a sneer. His moment of victory turned to a rage that screwed his facial features into a grimace.

When he stopped the vehicle and opened the door to get out, a dog blocked his forward progress. Dexter hesitated, unsure of his next move. *Is this mutt friendly?* He got the answer when the animal backed up, lowered his head, and growled.

He took a chance and started to get out of the car, moved slowly, planted a tentative step on the ground. There was another growl, this time so threatening Dexter heeded the warning and jerked his extended leg back inside the car. He slammed the door shut and stared down at the dog who had reared up on the side of the car, its nose about an inch away from the window.

There wasn't anything Dexter could do with that dog standing guard. He would have to come back later in the evening to make sure this was where Caron was staying. He had plenty to do for the rest of the day. He wanted to drive back to Russellville and rent a different car. The same vehicle seen around too often could cause a problem. He'd just tell them at the rental place there was a little skip in the engine and he didn't want to get stranded on his business trips.

The highway was a blur and he cursed each road sign that took him farther away from Caron. This was her fault. She was driving him to impose extenuating actions. Memory cards of the past fell into chronological order from the first time she had bumped into him at the deli and he saw the come-hither in her eyes to getting inside her Los Angeles apartment and running his hands through her stack of panties. That had caused a physical reaction.

His ire could not be controlled as he watched her interaction with a man she worked with and when she disappeared he went into panic mode. Persistence had its rewards when he got into her friend's apartment and found out where she had relocated. He flew across country to be near her.

The memory card show came to a sudden halt and was replaced by new images—another man. She dared to start seeing another man. Dexter refused to accept this new bump in his pursuit of the woman he loved. Doubts started to boil in resistance.

The battle of emotions warred inside his head as the

Russellville city limit sign came into view: one side pushing him to take aggressive action and win his woman once and for all, and the opposing force gaining credence that she rejected his company and insulted him by her association with this Trooper Bonner.

I'll give her another warning message. This time stronger. But how?

Dexter sat upright from his slouched position in the seat. *I'll show this state trooper what he's up against now that he's stuck his nose in my business. I'll take care of that damn dog and then I'll get her.*

CHAPTER 17

Caron sighed with relief. She was drying the last turkey before sliding it along the counter to Dot and a waiting oven baking bag and tablespoon of flour. Her attention to the chore at hand was put on pause for a more pleasant sight. Bill walked into the work area and headed in her direction. A couple of men called a friendly "Hey, Bill." He returned the greeting.

More than one female turned a head to observe his entrance. It had to have been the faded jeans and neatly tucked in plaid flannel shirt that initiated a rush of flurried weakness and caused her to lean a hip against the counter for support.

"How we doing? Got all those turkeys trussed up and ready to cook?" His grin made her heart spin like a toy top on a windy day. *I'm lucky to have met Bill Bonner.*

"Our part is done," she said. "Your timing is perfect." She went to the sink and gave her hands a good soapy cleansing.

"I got the calf comfortable in one of the barn stalls, but still need to scatter more bedding straw when we get to the farm. That shouldn't take long. Ready?"

"I'm ready to call it an afternoon. We got forty turkeys ready for baking. I was going to do the introductions, but this group already knows you."

Dot had finished bagging the last turkey and joined her at the sink to wash her hands. "Bill has volunteered his truck and time for civic club fundraisers and chaperoned youth groups on occasion. He's been a big help," she said.

This tidbit of information was not a surprise since he was at the church-sponsored community workday and hauling potatoes to farms. The knowledge further cemented her comfort and increased the level of trust. She was appreciative for the security Bill had brought back into her life. He helped people, but their relationship was more involved. Neither had mentioned the night of lovemaking. A silent understanding spiked between them and it was accepted as a moment of fulfilling need. She, however, could not prevent or deny the shiver of delightful memory that slid up her spine.

On the drive to the farm, Caron hummed with the music on the radio. The setting sun was displaying its final show of melding colors. *Life is good. I have truly been blessed meeting Bill. I feel safe and without question he is the best-looking guy who has ever been a part of my life, even Bruce. Bruce is an Adonis. Bill is more Vulcan.*

Token met them in the drive but when they got out she didn't wait around for the usual pat and rubs. She scampered to the bawling sound coming from the barn.

"Is it alright? It sounds like it's hurting."

Bill laughed. "He's alright."

The calf continued its cry of protest when they entered the barn, but settled down when Bill reached the stall. "He's sure enough weaned, but most likely still misses his mama. He'll be just fine when he goes to pasture and joins the others. I'm going up in the loft and pitch down a few more bales."

"I'll go with you."

"You first," he said and headed for a ladder fastened to a second-level platform.

Although climbing had never been a favorite activity, she went up the ladder with ease knowing Bill was behind. The aroma of fresh straw greeted and covered her with a ply of comfort. She settled and propped her elbows on a square bale to watch.

"This is a little haven away from the whole world. Uh— can I do anything?" She started to rise.

"This won't take but a jiffy." He smiled at her as he put on gloves, grabbed the binding wire on a bale, and shoved it from the loft. It dropped with a thud to the earthen hallway below. "A couple of bales will be plenty," he said.

He pushed over a final bale from the platform, removed a glove, and sat down beside her. The calf's bawling did not stop. "I'll scatter it around his stall. He'll settle down after he gets fed."

Caron watched him remove the other glove. Her voice echoed a serious tone. "Bill, I can't even begin to find the right words to express how much all this means to me."

He removed the other glove and brushed his knuckles against her cheek. The movement stirred the air around him and the seductive power of clean skin and male sweat released a shiver to run an unhindered course over her body.

Bill was watching her, his expression as serious as her words. "I don't know if you've noticed, but I care about and want to protect you. Caron, the little time we've known each other you've really made a difference in my world."

"You make it so easy, especially with all the garbage I'm bringing with me." A study of the late afternoon shadow on

ECHOES FROM THE MOUNTAIN

his face and the rough jaw gave her the confidence to close the distance between them and nuzzle against his shoulder.

"Come on. Let's finish this and head to the house," he said.

"I'm with you. Looking forward to a shower. I think I still smell raw turkey."

By the time Bill had spread straw in the stall and fed the calf, it was dark.

Token had been stretched out in a pile of loose straw outside the calf's stall, watching all the activity. "Token, you want to keep the calf company tonight?" Bill said. "It's up to you." A swishing tail disturbing the straw around her provided the answer.

As they walked to the house Caron tucked her hand in his. She was rewarded with a playful shoulder nudge.

* * *

DEXTER'S EYES stared at the road. One hand slid from the steering wheel and his fingers groped the cold package on the passenger's seat. The driveway to Bonner's house wasn't far. It was the midnight hour and time for him to warn off the man who had Caron in his house.

The plan was simple: pull into the driveway and throw out the present. Dogs couldn't resist raw meat and it hid the special additive Dexter put in the ground round. Obtaining the pesticide had been easy in an agriculture county with a stop by a farm supply store for a little surprise to mix in the bait.

"This is your *first* time in our store?" It was more of a statement from the counter clerk than a question.

"Yeah. I live over in the next county but knew I didn't have time to get back to my regular place before they closed. Something's eating on my roses and I wanted to take care of the problem before it got any worse." Dexter ended the sentence with a little grin.

The clerk cautioned him to keep the pesticide away from any pets or domesticated animals. "This should work. You a producer or home owner?"

Dexter wanted to shout back, "none of your business," but kept his voice calm with a noncommittal answer. "Only play in the backyard."

That explanation may have satisfied the employee, but in the silence, as he exited the store, Dexter knew the clerk had eyes on his back. That made him itch in discomfort and the possibility of being identified.

He slowed to ease into the driveway but only enough to get the vehicle off the road. The car's headlights picked up the dog's image running down the drive. Dexter moved fast, rolled down the window, threw out the package, and shifted in reverse to get the car back onto the pavement. As the car moved forward on the road, a brief glance in the side mirror picked up the image of the dog, head drooped and inspecting the package. Dexter accelerated the car to get out of the area.

A belch of stomach gas erupted into his mouth, eager to be released. Its odor made him press his lips together to squash a gag. It had been hours since his last meal, his purpose overriding any desire to eat. His moods became a yoyo of emotion, moving from anger to excitement with each mile he put between him and the house that held his love. The madness reached a boiling point but then excitement made a rebound when he thought of the hurt he would cause the man by giving the dog a good dose of pesticide.

It was all Caron's fault. She was making him take drastic measures. The dog was a path to warn off the man.

Dexter wanted the man to suffer and rue his involvement in a relationship that was none of his business. Caron belonged to him and he would go anywhere and initiate any measures to make sure no other man enjoyed her beauty or the delights her body promised.

CHAPTER 18

"Molly's idea of preparing a meal is to cook so much food the table bows in the center. I was invited to Thanksgiving dinner last year," Bill said as they stepped down the porch steps and moved toward Truck. Caron responded to his light mood with her own laugh.

"Wonder if Token is still with the calf? I missed her company last night." She scoured the area, her search stopping at the barn.

"She probably stayed in the barn last night, what with something new in her territory," Bill said. "Give me a minute. I'll take some feed down to her." He turned around and went back into the house.

Caron slowed her steps and waited by Truck, watched as Bill returned with a dish of food and strolled leisurely toward the barn. He wasn't gone long.

"She's not in the barn, probably out for a morning run. She'll be okay. Molly always sends her a special treat, and somehow Token knows and meets me in the driveway." Caron couldn't ignore the deepening wrinkles across his forehead, nor did she miss the target of his focus across the outlying pastures.

They got in Truck and about halfway down the drive Bill slammed his foot on the brake and jumped out of the pickup so fast Caron's hands landed against the dashboard to brace against the sudden stop. The reason registered when she saw him go to his knees in the shallow ditch. She bounced out of her seat and ran around the front of the vehicle.

"No." Caron dropped to the ground beside Bill. Token was trying to stand but her quivering legs couldn't support the weight. Her head rested in Bill's left hand, while his other one searched the length of her body.

"Nothing seems to be broken. Her breathing is shallow." Token whimpered. Her body wrenched.

"What's wrong, baby? What's that?" His attention homed in on the tattered package, partially hidden in the dead weeds a few feet away. He eased Token's head back to the ground and closed the distance to squat over the ripped paper, picked up a stick and poked around the remains. "Damn."

Caron remained on her knees beside Token. "What is it?"

Bill reached into his jacket pocket and pulled out a cell phone. There was a pause.

"Dale. This is Bill Bonner. I'm sorry it being Thanksgiving but this is an emergency. Token has been poisoned." There was a moment of hesitation. "Yeah, I'll meet you at the clinic."

The sob that tore from Caron's throat was accompanied by a flood of tears. "Please—no," she said.

Bill grabbed gloves and a blanket from the back of Truck. He retrieved what was left of the package and tossed it on the pickup bed. The blood red in his cheeks was as solid as new brick, fresh from the kiln. His jaws were set so hard Caron thought she could hear teeth grind. Danger signs glittered in his eyes.

"What can I do?" Caron said.

"Get in Truck. I'll put Token in front."

Caron hurried. Bill was right behind and started to spread the blanket on the seat. "Put it on my lap." Bill lifted Token from the ditch and carried her to the truck. He laid her in Caron's waiting arms.

She tucked the blanket close. Her arms encircled the jerking body. She rocked Token in an attempt at reassurance. Drool from Token's mouth was so thick it clung to her bottom lip. Caron tried to wipe it away on the blanket corner and in moving Token's head she stared into big brown eyes. Caron's heart ached at what she saw. It was imperative her voice remain soft and calm. She mumbled words of encouragement.

Bill had said nothing since they got in Truck, but when he did speak, each word forced from his mouth was accented with knowledge. His lips barely moved.

"She's been poisoned. I recognized those pellets in the meat. Not all of them had dissolved. Someone threw out hamburger meat with a pesticide in it."

Caron did not look up, but knew they were traveling at an accelerated speed. She kept her face close to Token's ear. Tears she could not stop fell into the soft hair. Her soothing words did not stop. "Pretty baby, it's going to be okay. We love you." She looked up again when the truck slid to a stop. Bill wasted no time. He was out of the pickup, and opened her door to gather Token in his arms. Caron ran to keep up with his loping strides. The veterinarian was waiting in the lobby.

"I've got some of the stuff she ate," Bill said. The vet took Token from Bill and started walking toward another room.

"Get it. Let's be sure. Hurry. I've got everything set up in the lab."

Caron stood aside to give each man a clear path, but she

wouldn't allow Token out of her sight. She followed the vet into a small room where he placed Token on a metal table and picked up a small shaver. A patch of hair on Token's leg was zipped away and a syringe inserted to draw blood. Caron leaned over. "It's going to be okay. We're not going to leave you." Her hands caressed the length of Token's body as she spoke.

Bill returned with the remains of what Token had eaten and stood beside her.

The vet removed the syringe and took the package. "I'm going to run tests. It'll take about fifteen minutes."

Bill joined Caron, leaned close to Token and gently rubbed his fingers down the length of her nose. "We're here, pretty girl." Token tried to lift her head and respond to his touch but the move was too much for her. Her head dropped back on the shiny metal.

"Oh, Bill, she's got to be all right. Oh please, Lord, let her be okay." Caron could not stop the sob that wanted release from her throat. She could feel the side of Bill's body touching hers. It was stiff, hard as cement.

He pulled out the phone and made another call. "Matt— Bill. We won't be over for dinner."

Caron was privy to one side of the conversation, but it took no imagination to understand.

"Someone poisoned Token. We're at Dale's clinic and he's running tests. We may be here a while. Yeah, I'll call and give you an update as soon as I know."

It was the longest fifteen minutes Caron had ever experienced and she knew if she was impatient it had to be an onus of worry on Bill.

Both their heads jerked when the door opened and the vet returned. The expression on his face told them nothing. He held a sheet of paper in his hand.

"It's disulfoton, a common pesticide. I'm going to start an IV antidote to stabilize her heart rate."

"How long before we know if it's working?"

"Not long."

He injected a needle and syringe of solution into the IV.

"Dale, this is Caron Kimball. Caron, Dr. Dale Moore."

Caron acknowledged him. She said nothing. Her throat was so full of emotion any effort to speak would have been a sob. Her attention was fixated on the stethoscope in Dr. Moore's hand and its motion as it moved to check Token's breathing.

"Where did she get the meat?" he asked.

"Someone threw it out in the ditch that runs along the driveway. Had to be last night. It wasn't there when we arrived home yesterday."

"Do you think it was done on purpose?"

"I don't know."

Time crawled. Caron was convinced the hands on the wall clock were broken. Bill's arm found its way around her shoulders.

"Her heartbeat and breathing are more stable. She's still pretty weak. I'm going to add another treatment in the IV." He left the room and returned with another syringe that he injected in Token's IV tube.

The waiting continued.

"Dale, I owe you big time. I'm so sorry I pulled you in on a holiday," Bill said.

"It's part of the job. That's what friends do. We were going to do dinner later anyway—waiting on Debbie to drive up from the university."

"Token has been a big part of my life since I moved here. I think we needed each other. Still do. Caron has been added to the family." His hand, still resting on her shoulder, tightened. Bill's voice dropped a level as he said, "Is Token going to be okay?"

"She's pretty weak, but is responding. It'll be a while. Bill, if she'd eaten more of the meat she wouldn't have made it. Good thing you found her and didn't wait around to get her to me."

"Can I take her home?"

"Hmm...maybe in a few hours."

"I don't want to leave her." Bill looked at his watch. "Dale, you've got a Thanksgiving dinner to go to."

"Token is resting comfortably," the vet said. "Why don't we do this. I'll go have dinner with the family. I'm just a couple of minutes away if you need me. Ya'll stay with Token. I'll come back after dinner and if she's continuing to improve you can take her home. But you will need to keep her inactive and quiet for a couple of days."

"Thanks, Doc. I feel better staying with her."

Caron listened, agreeing silently.

"We'll both stay," she said.

Bill's hand responded with a shoulder squeeze.

"I'll see ya'll in a little while. We should know more by then," Dale said.

When he left, Bill pulled two chairs close to the metal table so they could sit, near enough to reach and give Token reassuring pats.

"I've never been so scared. Bill, you're so lucky to have Dr. Moore as your vet."

"The advantages of living in a smaller community and knowing folks."

Her upper body sagged with a bit of relief and she welcomed the new expression on his face. The tight muscles in his cheeks eased.

"Who would be so mean to do this?"

Bill placed his hand on Token's head. "I don't know. There are people who get their kicks from hurting others."

Caron crossed her arms to rest along the edge of the table. They touched against Token's paws. She leaned forward and cushioned her head, closed her eyes and prayed a silent thank you that Token's life had been spared. She was grateful Bill did not lose his beloved pet. Her eyes remained closed.

A pinprick of possibilities started to grow and surged through her body, heat so intense she reacted and jolted upright, her back rigid with fear. It was so sudden, Bill's hand stopped stroking Token and his attention switched to her.

"Do you think the stalker could be responsible for this? I believe he's crazy, but this is totally insane."

"That thought had entered my mind. There are three farm supply stores in the county. I'll get in touch with Wallace. They might have surveillance systems. I'll be off this weekend and can check them out."

"Oh, Bill, what have I done? I'm so sorry to get you involved in my problem and now Token has been hurt. This maniac went after my friend Bruce, and now you." She covered her face with both hands.

He pulled her hands apart and pressed them in a prayerful clasp.

"Now, you look at me." His hands kept hers covered.

Caron lifted her head.

"This is not your fault. It may or may not have been this man who's harassing you. The main thing is, Token is going to be okay."

"But what about tomorrow? We have to be back at work."

"I'll put her in the stall with the new calf. They can keep each other company."

"It's going to be a long day. Maybe there won't be much going on at the office since it's after Thanksgiving and the

ECHOES FROM THE MOUNTAIN

first big shopping day. I'll try to get back to the farm early. If this works out, do you want me to bring Token into the house?"

"I don't want you to be out there on the highway alone. There's no way I can leave work early. It'll be a big traffic day with shoppers jamming the highways in and out of the city. I'll be in as soon as the report is done."

"I'll be careful. You can't possibly be with me every moment. I promise to stay alert and watch all four directions when I'm in the car."

"I should be in by five-thirty. You and Token stay inside the house until I get here. I've been thinking about a protection for you. We'll talk about it." He took the cell phone out of his shirt pocket and tapped the screen. The pause was short.

"Matt, Token is going to be okay. Everything is under control. Thanks for the offer. Yeah, Dale says to keep her activities limited…waiting for the okay to take her home. Well, I don't know exactly what time we'll get back to the farm. Thanks for inviting us. I'm thankful Token is going to be okay. …You too, Matt. Talk to you later."

Caron jumped when the door to their waiting room swung open.

"Now, let's see how she's doing. I'm going to do another blood test." Dr. Moore inserted the syringe and Token raised her head. "It's okay, girl. I won't stick you anymore after we get this sample. Bill, it'll take a few minutes to run through the test. I want to be sure before she goes home."

He exited into a hallway and Caron could hear movement and soft clinking. Her hand caressed Token's side. Time did not stand still. When they had first arrived and Token's life was threatened, hands on the wall clock were stuck in limbo. With the knowledge Token would be okay, the heavy cloud of waiting lifted.

The slight smile on Dr. Moore's face was what they wanted to see when he came back into the room. "She's coming along fine and can go home but remember to keep her activities limited. There's going to be a bit of weakness."

"How much, Dale?" Bill pulled out his billfold.

"I'll have Marcy do some figuring and send you a bill," he said.

Caron got the blanket. Bill lifted Token from the table. She did not resist. "Thanks, Dale. You saved her life."

Dr. Moore followed them through the lobby and opened the entrance door.

When they got to Truck, Caron spread the blanket across her lap. "Put her here."

As they drove out of the parking lot, Caron's mood turned happier and Bill's long sigh was encouraging. His wrinkles were softer. They covered the distance to the farm in thankful silence.

When they stopped in the drive, Bill got out, came around to her side and lifted Token. "You go ahead and open the door," he said.

"What's that?" Caron asked, pointing to a large white container on the front porch.

"Let's get Token inside and we'll see."

Token had started to squirm in his arms and he set her down in the living room.

He stepped back to the container, bent over, lifted a corner of the lid and then removed it entirely. A big grin spread his lips and a low chuckle followed.

"Looks like the chuck wagon came by while we were gone."

Caron could not see what was inside the container that was so amusing.

"Matt and Molly brought over Thanksgiving," he said.

"And a lot of it," he added. His chuckle turned into full-

ECHOES FROM THE MOUNTAIN

blown laughter. "Molly sure didn't want us to go hungry." He lifted the container and carted it inside.

Caron was right behind him as he made his way to the kitchen.

"I hope you're hungry," Bill said as he put the box on the table and started unloading the contents. They stood back and looked at the spread of food blanketing the table. He pulled out his cell phone. Caron smiled. She knew who he was calling.

"Matt, you and Molly are too much. We just got home. Thanks to both of you for all the food. ...Well, I assure you we're going to make a dent in it tonight. There'll be enough leftovers to last for days. ...You bet, Matt. We'll be seeing ya'll soon."

"I've never seen so much food in one container," Caron said. "I'll get plates."

Knowing Token had survived the attempt on her life whet their appetites. Each sealed dish was uncovered and the kitchen was filled with a flurry of appreciative words and compliments for Molly's culinary talents. They devoured mashed potatoes, gravy, turkey, ham, dressing, and with each morsel eaten more reactions for the bounty.

Token pushed against Caron's leg. "Can she have a taste of turkey?"

"Dale didn't say not to feed her. I'm sure one little bite won't hurt."

Token took the strip of meat from Caron's hand, gobbled it down, and looked up. "That's all you can have tonight, pretty girl." Token settled back down on the floor beside her feet.

Caron chewed the last bite on her plate and pushed the chair back a little. "That's it. I can't eat another bite. If I do, I'll explode. I'll save dessert for later."

"Right there with you. It sure was good."

"I admire women who can go into a kitchen and turn out a plethora of culinary delights. My mom could. I'll never be able to follow her example," Caron said.

"Your talents run in a different direction," Bill said.

"Can Token stay with me tonight?"

"If you're comfortable with her being there."

"Comfortable? Yes." *I'm comfortable with both Token and you —maybe too comfortable, but my heart says it's right.* Before she closed her eyes to sleep there would be another prayer, thankful Token was going to be okay and ask for protection from the evil intent that lurked so near.

CHAPTER 19

Bill slid his legs to the edge of the bed and got up. He retrieved his phone from the nightstand and made a barefooted path to the kitchen to start the coffee brewing. His shoulders scrunched in a rotation movement to wake up cramped muscles. It had been a restless toss-and-turn night and a relief when he saw the first daylight seep between the Venetian blind slats. Any contemplated movement was put on pause, however, while he waited for the coffee to finish trickling into the carafe. A full cup in hand, he lifted it to his mouth but before taking the first sip allowed the faint wisp of hot steam to tease. He inhaled the aroma and closed his eyes to savor the moment.

His footsteps remained silent as he made his way to the living room and sat down on the sofa. With cup in one hand and phone in the other, he leaned forward to rest an elbow on each knee, flipped open the phone, pressed a tab and waited, but not long.

"Wallace. Bill. …wanted to catch you early." He listened to the husky reply. "No problem. Got some coffee in me. Let's talk. Have you found out anything?"

"We've had patrols in the area of Caron's apartment—nothing out of the ordinary. This dude is diabolically smart. He's not exactly leaving any shoe prints for us to follow. I'm betting he's using burner phones. I've checked out the local car rentals. Nothing there. Will get to others in surrounding areas."

"Wallace, someone tried to poison Token."

"Is she okay?" His voice changed from its professional authority to a softer, more concerned inflection.

"We got her to the vet in time. She'll be weak for a few days. I'm going to keep her pretty close."

"What happened?"

"Someone threw out hamburger in the driveway entrance chock full of pesticide. Token got into it. Dr. Moore said we got her to him just in time."

"Are you thinking this stalker had anything to do with it?"

"Caron said he made threats against her co-worker in Los Angeles over their friendship."

"If it was him, he had to buy that stuff here and its only available at farm supply stores."

"I'm off tomorrow. How about I visit the places around here and see what washes out—check security videos if they have them. I want to do something."

"Go for it. That'll give me more time to check out the car rentals. I'm also checking on incoming flights from California, but we don't know exactly when this dude arrived. He's not staying in this area—haven't found anyone from California registered in the motels. We're going to extend our search. How's Caron doing?"

"She's hanging in there. I'm staying pretty close and keep reminding her to stay alert to surroundings and not travel in isolated places. So far, so good."

"Is this a big brother syndrome or is it turning into something more?"

Bill paused before he spoke. "Hey, wasn't looking for a friendship nor relationship, but it's developing." He listened to Wallace's soft laugh.

"Yeah, Cupid has a way of shooting arrows when we least expect it."

A grin spread and lifted the corner of Bill's lips. "Looks like I didn't dodge in time."

Wallace chuckled. "I'll stay in touch and let you know what I find out."

"Likewise."

"By the way, have you thought about her having a little protection when you're not around?"

"I have been meaning to talk to her about that," Bill said. He ended the call and drained the last bit of coffee from the cup, got up and went back into the kitchen for a refill. He needed to wake Caron. There hadn't been any movement from the bedroom and Token might need to go outside.

He poured a second mug of coffee and balanced them both at elbow height as he walked toward Caron's bedroom, but stopped so abruptly the hot liquid sloshed onto his hand. A quick lick of his tongue removed the coffee and nursed the sting. He glanced at the closed bedroom door then studied the containers in his hands. Not a muscle in his body moved. A thought kept him from taking the next step. *Am I being presumptuous to enter the bedroom?*

The corners of his mouth lifted. His head inched side-to-side in disbelief as to what he was doing—carrying morning coffee to a woman sleeping in a bedroom next to his. The door nudged open when he pushed against it with his big toe.

The sight that greeted him dismissed any regrets and filled his heart with such an intense flood of airy lightness he came to a halt and leaned against the doorframe. He wanted to stand and devour the scene. In the dim light his eyes feasted on Caron cuddled against Token.

He placed the extra cup on the adjacent dresser and allowed his eyes to see the beauty and reality of the moment. It wasn't a shock because he had come to realize and accept she was filling the vacancy in his life. His breathing deepened and became a bit ragged as the memory of the intimate night they shared replayed in his mind. She had wanted him, needed the assurance that only a human touch could provide in the chaos of a traumatic situation. All he had wanted was to cover her with emotional security, but the sparks of passion that had lain fallow in his body rose and desired an outlet.

In the morning he had apologized, but Caron did not express regrets for their lovemaking. It had been accepted and tucked away. He wanted her safe and had ensconced her in his home and life. It was a matter of his coming in, out of the cold, and finding a blazing warmth. There would be a time and place in the future for the physical relationship, but first the stalker had to be caught and put away.

Movement on the bed drew his attention back to the present. Token lifted her head, looked in his direction, jumped off the bed, and hurried to where he stood. The movement awoke Caron. "Token?"

"She's probably bursting to get outside. I'm sure she didn't want to give up her warm spot next to you." He grinned and set his cup on the dresser, retrieved hers and carried it to her. "Be right back."

Bill hurried to let a dancing Token out the back patio door. He watched as she scurried to the hedge and squatted to relieve herself. When she finished he opened the door and called. "Come, pretty girl. You're going to have to stay close for a few days." Token had stopped and looked up to her master and did not hesitate to go back inside when he opened the door. They headed back to Caron's bedroom. Token asserted her claim beside Caron who was now sitting up in the middle of the bed and sipping from the cup. Bill walked toward the bed but stopped at the edge.

"Good coffee," she said. "Come—sit."

She patted the edge of the bed and moved to give him room. Token didn't budge or offer to give up her space, which brought a resounding laugh from Bill. "She's not going to cede any territory. What have you done to my dog?"

"We have to stick together."

"I've been talking to Wallace. Caught him before he went to work and got involved with the day. There are no definite leads. Your stalker is covering his tracks well. I've been meaning to discuss something with you." He turned to make sure they directly faced each other.

"This sounds serious."

"It is. How do you feel about guns? Would you carry one with you if I get it?"

The coffee cup stopped halfway to her mouth. He had her attention.

"I've never thought about carrying a gun. Do you think it's necessary? Do you think this man is that dangerous?"

"He broke into your apartment, threatened your friend. He's followed you from Los Angeles, almost three thousand miles and may be responsible for poisoning Token. Yes, I think he's that dangerous—mentally unstable."

"I've never shot a gun."

"I'll teach you."

"What about pepper spray?" she said.

"You can carry that in your purse until we can do some gun safety and target practice. We need to get you a license to carry. Think about it. You need to have protection. I may not always be with you." He eased up from the bed. "Tomorrow I'm going to visit the farm supply stores. Hopefully, they'll have security systems. Maybe something will show up. Token, come. I'm putting you in the stall with the calf for the day." She hopped off the bed and followed him out of the room.

Caron finished her coffee, appreciating the fact that she had been served in bed, and hurried to the bathroom. She washed her face, brushed her teeth, and was back in her bedroom when she heard the sounds of Bill returning and shower water splashing.

Putting on makeup, she asked herself would she be comfortable carrying a gun? The idea of keeping a can of pepper spray in her purse or near was more preferable. *Am I becoming too reliant on Bill?* He almost lost his beloved Token because of her. She could not erase the guilt of it being her fault. It wouldn't have happened if Bill wasn't trying to be her protector. Maybe it was time for her to admit the danger to anything and anybody close to her and be responsible for her own safety. Perhaps a gun was the answer.

She waited for him in the living room. When he stepped through the door her heart skipped a beat.

"I've got to swing by the apartment and put these clothes in the washer. Bill, I can't stay here forever. I have to think about returning to the apartment. You've been more than generous and there are extra patrols around the area."

He stopped in the middle of the living room, legs slightly parted, hands clasped in the back, standing upright and solid as a bedpost. She wanted to throw out a line and pull back the words that had come out of her mouth. The authority he commanded resonated around the room.

"I'd feel better if you stayed the weekend—at least until I see if anything turns up at the farm supply stores." She could not even guess what he was thinking and the stone-faced expression provided no hint. His words, however, were quiet and spoken with a distinctive connotation.

"Why don't I stop by that outdoor equipment store in

town and buy a can of pepper spray, at least until we have more time to talk about me carrying a gun."

Bill had not moved and Caron began to think he would continue to protest her return to the apartment. When he spoke his concentrated vision was directed straight to her eyes while his mouth, downturned at the corners, almost made her say she would stay at the farm.

"Do you promise to stop by and get that pepper spray? And I'll stop by the apartment after my shift ends and we'll see how your day went. You won't take any unnecessary trips, will you?"

"I promise. It'll probably be one boring day with everyone out shopping anyway, but it'll give me some time to do desk work."

"I don't know how close I'll be to the city and if I can meet you for lunch. A lot depends on the shopper traffic."

"I'll order in and only go by and pick it up."

"Okay. I'll follow you in to work and see you at the apartment after my shift ends."

They walked from the house. Bill followed her to her vehicle and opened the door before climbing into Truck. He gave a solemn wave as she inserted the key and the motor hummed to life. She smiled and returned the gesture.

A bit of apprehension crowded into the front seat beside her, but it was dismissed as she pulled onto the highway. Bill followed.

The distance into town zipped by in no time. A smile broke across her mouth as she acknowledged that familiarity with the terrain shortened the trip.

The routine had been established—park and he escorted her to the front door of the newspaper building. "I'll see you at the apartment after my shift ends?" He placed his hands on her shoulders. "Now don't forget to pick up the pepper spray and be careful."

He opened the door. She stepped inside and went up the steps to the editorial staff offices, but stopped to fill a coffee cup before she settled at the desk. The intercom on her phone buzzed.

She leaned back in the chair as her free hand lifted the receiver and pressed it against her ear. "Caron Kimball."

"How's the dog?"

CHAPTER 20

Caron could not breathe. Her mouth flew open to suck in more air. The raspy voice crawled from the telephone receiver. Danger flashed through her brain.

"Cat got your tongue?" A snicker followed. "How's the dog?"

Adrenalin fed her anger. "You—why did you hurt Token?"

"Just a little message to your friend. He's messing with something that belongs to me—you."

Defiant words exploded in response. "Never. Never! I do not know you. I do not want to know you. I do not want anything to do with you." She screamed at the receiver. Jennifer walked into the room, came to an abrupt halt, and stared. "Leave me alone. Stay away from my friends."

"You started this at that deli—bumped into me and acted like it was an accident. I knew better. I knew what you wanted. You started the game. It's the chase. Now, you don't want to *hide* from me, do you?" The question was reduced to a suggestive whisper. "I've got something you want."

Jennifer came into the room, eased to her desk and sat

down, but her attention remained on Caron. Vicki walked in and stopped half way across the room. Her attention went from Caron to Jennifer."

The anger in Caron's voice was accented with sharp jabs. "You're insane!" The laugh through the receiver dumped a bucket of ice cubes on her earlobe and the low snicker grew to a high-pitched cackle. *He is crazy.*

"Leave me alone! Leave my friends alone!"

She lowered her voice a notch but kept the tone serious and on point. "You're going to be caught. We met with an investigator. They're hunting for you this very minute. They'll catch you and you'll be charged! You're going to answer for your insidious stalking, and poisoning Token."

"Who do you think you're messing with, *little girl*. I'm sure you'd hate to see anything happen to that state trooper. You just better hope I don't change my mind about *you*. I am getting a little tired of this chase."

Caron sat back down. Her cramped muscles refused to give up their tense state. She leaned forward and propped her elbows on the desk. Her fingers gripped the receiver so hard they were pale white. "You can threaten all you want. I will never want anything to do with you. You belong in a mental institution."

The voice went silent but she could still hear his panting breath. It became so loud and oppressive she wanted to gag. "You're sick! You're a coward! Don't call me again."

As she moved the receiver from her ear, she heard the shout of anger. "I'll show you who's a coward."

She stared at the phone and tried to calm her thoughts, find some meaning to what she had just heard. A new fear sparked and started to grow. The realization cut deep when she considered the potential harm that could touch Bill—already Token. Even co-workers could be put in danger for their association with her. The chill of this knowledge raked on her nerves and magnified as she looked across the room to Jennifer and Vicki.

They remained silent but their focus on Caron had not let up.

, aron had to get her emotions under control before speaking. It was no longer a choice to keep silent. The story had to be told. The publisher needed to know. They all had to know about the stalker.

"Jennifer, Vicki, I have something to share with you."

They did not interrupt as Caron told them about the deli incident in Los Angeles and finally being forced to leave California. She had to get away from the stalker. Her friend, Bruce, had gone to college with the publisher's son and got her the job in North Fork. She was hopeful the move would alleviate the stalker's attention and she could eventually return to California. When she finished, silence resonated in the room so heavy it would have required a sharp-edged knife to slice open a door and let in fresh air.

Vicki spoke first, in a low voice, her full attention on Caron. "You have to tell Mr. Wilson."

"I thought I had left this all behind in California. I just hope it doesn't affect my job."

"He'll understand," Vicki said. "He's a good guy."

"After I went to the Farm City Banquet with Bill Bonner and the four flat tires incident, it has all been downhill. Bill insisted I would be safer at his farm—give authorities time to start an investigation. The stalker poisoned Bill's dog. He said so on the phone. We spent Thanksgiving at the vet."

"She's going to be alright—right? You have got to tell the publisher," Jennifer said.

"There were more threats this morning. I don't want anyone to get hurt because of me."

Caron lifted the receiver and tapped the intercom numbers for Mr. Wilson's office. "I need to talk with you, Mr. Wilson. Do you have time?"

"Come on," he said.

He listened while Caron repeated the story again. The only sound in the room was a muted squeak from rollers on his chair when it inched backward. He propped both elbows on the desk. Caron had his full attention. When she finished and sat silent, the publisher crossed his arms and leaned forward in his chair.

"Caron, my son told me why you had to make the move—not all the details, but I was aware of the circumstances. His friend filled him in on the situation. I'll talk to the police chief."

She told him about Bill Bonner. A blush covered her face when she mentioned he had offered her a safe haven at his farm. There was no judgmental expression on her employer's face.

"I know Bill—good man. We may need to confine your movements for a while?"

"We met with Bill's friend Wallace at the police department. He's investigating."

"That's good."

"Bill's dog was poisoned. It was the stalker. He admitted it this morning."

"Caron, let's limit your outside assignments for a while. At least until they can get a handle on this stalker. Do interviews by telephone. Vicki and Jennifer can help with photos when they're needed. It will be safer. You said Bill follows you in to town and back to the farm?"

"He does."

"Then it's settled."

"I'm sorry to cause all this trouble. Thank you for the

support. Mr. Wilson, I want this to be over, too. I want my life back to normal."

"Just remember, stay in or near the office and make sure people are around if you do have to go out."

When she got back to her desk, Vicki and Jennifer waited for her to get settled and tell them how the meeting went.

"Then it's settled. We'll help get you past this thing. If Trooper Bonner can't be with you at lunch, we'll make plans for you to be with one of us. Between me and Jennifer we'll take any photos you need," Vicki said.

"Thanks. This means so much. I worry about Bill's safety, the farm. It's my fault Token was poisoned."

"It will all pass," Jennifer said. "Is your trooper meeting you for lunch?"

My trooper. The grin inside broke free.

"There was no way he could know how close he'd be today with holiday shopping traffic. I promised I'd go by the gun shop and buy some pepper spray. He wants me to learn how to shoot a gun. I'm not comfortable with that, but I can handle the spray."

"We'll take care of that if he doesn't get back in town."

The remainder of the morning crept along at a snail's pace. She jumped when the buzz from her cell phone interrupted the silence. *Oh, please let it be Bill.* The display window on the phone flashed "Bill."

"Caron, I'm not going to be near enough to meet you for lunch."

"That's okay. I'll have lunch with Vicky and Jennifer. I had to tell them what was going on¾also the publisher. I had to. Bill, he called here this morning."

She heard a long, steady breath of air. "Tell me about it."

"He admitted to poisoning Token."

Bill's response was instant and sharp. "He has to be stopped."

"He made more threats, and included you. Bill, I'm so sorry. You're patrolling out there on the highway alone. There's no telling what this idiot may try."

"Don't you worry. I'm more than he can handle any time. He's the type who won't come face-to-face—nothing more than a coward who has to sneak around in the darkness. I wish he would face me."

"I'm angry. He hurt Token. I know you love her, but so do I."

"Tomorrow I'll visit the farm supply stores. Local folks are regulars. A new customer wanting a pesticide would pretty much stand out. Maybe something will show up if they have security systems. We'll get a break—one is all I want. I want you to go with me. Maybe something will jar your memory if we can get a look at any of the tapes."

"The publisher suggested I do interviews over the phone and limit outside activities. Jennifer and Vicki volunteered to take any photos I may need. We're going by to pick up that pepper spray when we go to lunch."

"Are you going to be okay?"

"Sure, but it makes me fighting mad that he's causing pain to the people I care about."

A lazy chuckle drifted out of the receiver. "The same caring you have for your friend Bruce?"

She paused to search for the right words and chose to be candid.

"I was never intimate with Bruce. I never wanted Bruce to share my bed. My feelings for you are *very* different from the friendship I have with Bruce." *There, I said it.*

Dead silence.

"Are you sure you want to continue in the direction this conversation is taking?" he asked.

"It would appear fate has already made that decision," she answered.

"Then I'll be honest. I want more than your friendship. The first night we met I knew you were special." He stopped talking for only a second. "This is a heck of a way to be having this conversation—over the phone."

There were no regrets for her next statement.

"Would you care to continue it at a more convenient time and place." *I've never been this forward with anyone.*

"You can count on it," he said.

* * *

DEXTER MUMBLED the words through clenched teeth pressed so tight his jaws hurt as he pulled onto the highway and headed out of town. "After I get through with her, she won't be fit for anyone."

His heart pounded hard and fast against taut chest muscles. A face red with contemptible rage confronted him in the rearview mirror. "I'll show her who's a coward."

He thought throwing out a little "treat" to the dog would announce his determination to claim her as his woman. There was no remorse in her voice when he talked with her on the phone. There was nothing but total disregard for his obvious devotion. She did not confess it was a game of wanting him to run after her.

The pain of rejection screamed for revenge. Images of Caron on her knees and begging forgiveness raced through his brain with a picture of the end in sight.

He must get her away from that state trooper. How? She would have to be taken somewhere to give him privacy. This was farming country with more than one old, vacant barn on an isolated landscape. There would be one to fill the need. All he had to do was search and find the right one. Then he would have plenty of time to assert his will¾give her a taste of the pain she had inflicted on him. Another look into the rearview mirror and he admired the smile that spread across his lips and the new calm that ran through his body.

"She's dead. I'm finished with her. I'll wait for the right time. I'll show her who's a coward."

CHAPTER 21

Caron did not want to surrender the euphoria of awakening in Bill's bed. Her eyes remained closed as she was unwilling to relinquish the aura of warmth. The physical bliss made her burrow deeper into the thick blanket. Their lovemaking had been passionate. He made her complete. A slight jar on the edge of the bed and lifting of weight made her peek. She did not try to stifle the smile that tickled her lips.

Satisfaction ran through every vein as she feasted on the full image of Bill as he walked toward the dresser. She opted to be still and soak in the view. Her eyes were partially closed but there was enough vision through the squints to observe his progress to the corner of the room and watch him slide long, muscled legs into sweat pants. He secured the front tie before turning in her direction. Caron remained motionless but opened both eyes.

"You're beautiful," he said.

"My view of you walking across the room isn't so bad either."

"I'll go put on the coffee, Sleeping Beauty."

"Thank you, sweet prince. I'm going to take a shower." She bounced out of bed and started toward the bathroom. A long arm reached out and stopped her progress. Another arm encircled her waist and pulled her close. She became a willing prisoner.

"Do you know how much you mean to me? I was so ready to accept living out the rest of my life alone. You have given me the chance for happiness again," he said.

Demanding barks interrupted the moment. He pulled back but still nibbled at her lips.

"I think Token is tired of barn confinement. I'll put on coffee and go let her out."

Caron was reluctant to give up her position and let him know by a soft, vocal protest, but conceded. "Hm. Okay. Go get the baby. She wants you, too."

"That includes you?" His focus never left her face as he put on a T-shirt and shoved bare feet into moccasins.

"That's a definite yes." She inched her arms around his waist.

One arm held her in his embrace and a free hand pressed her face against his chest. She savored the touch but took a half step back. "Go get Token, but not before you put on coffee.

She stepped into the shower and streams of water soaked her from head to toe. Thoughts of the previous night washed over her skin as water trickled paths to search and fill hidden crevices.

The conversation they promised to have about their relationship did not occur. When they arrived at the farm and got out of their vehicles, he reached for her hand and held it until they got inside. They were so close his heat radiated onto her cheeks. His hands inched up her arms, slid along her shoulders, and continued up her neck. They did not stop moving until his palms pressed flat against her cheeks.

There were no words. He tilted her head so she would have a full view of his face. His eyes were a reflection of burning passion.

"Do you want to talk?"

Her body was trembling so hard she had to lean into him for support.

In one smooth dip she was being carried to the bedroom.

Sweet memories of the passion that consumed and united them swept away all thought of conversation and the dark cloud that loomed outside the front door. For long minutes in their isolated world of lovemaking, the stalker ceased to exist.

Bill was pouring coffee by the time she dressed and made it to the kitchen. Token met her halfway across the room, and nudged against her leg. Caron dropped to her knees. She stretched her arms around Token's neck and pulled her close. "I'm so thankful you're okay, pretty baby." That got her one big, sloppy lick on the face.

Caron's attention moved from Token to Bill. He had propped against the counter to watch. His expression was one of pure delight, a sight she could get used to.

"She and I have a mutual agreement on what we like," he said and handed her a cup of coffee. She carried it to the breakfast nook and sat down.

"We need to get a move on. The farm supply stores open early. Everyone tries to finish up chores on the weekend and get supplies to start off Monday. There's three locations. I know some of the employees. They'll tell me if any unfamiliar face has bought pesticides lately."

Bill was silent as he joined her at the table and lifted his cup to take a slow sip of coffee. She looked into eyes that were fixed in a steady beam on her face.

"I'm tired of looking over my shoulder," she said.

"We'll get him. His luck will run out and I'll be there when it does." That low, pronounced statement was issued from lips that were almost motionless. The words were firm and calculated. "While we're out, I want to look over the gun inventories. How about I buy breakfast?"

"I can handle that. And the guns, remember I've never shot one."

"I'll teach you. We'll set up targets here at the farm so you can practice. While you finish your coffee, I'll get Token back to the barn."

"She's not going to like being shut up again," Caron said. Token heard her name, lifted her ears, got up and crept to Bill. "I think she knows you're going to put her back in the stall."

Bill bent over and put his hands on each side of Token's jowls and massaged with his fingers. "I know you don't like being shut up, but, pretty girl, I don't want you getting into trouble again. We'll catch that man who hurt you. That's a promise."

Caron's insides melted as she watched Bill reassure Token and listened to the soft words.

"Come on, baby, let's go. Won't take but a jiffy and I'll be back for a quick shower."

She finished her coffee and put their coffee cups in the sink. "I'll wash them when we get back," she said in a low, promising voice.

On the way into town, Caron's phone hummed. It was Bruce.

"Hope I didn't catch you too early."

"What a great surprise." She paused. "What's up? Is everything alright?"

"Thought I'd surprise you with a little visit."

"You're joking. You're coming to North Fork?" She had half turned to look at Bill as she spoke. He did not look at her. His face was a bland mask.

ECHOES FROM THE MOUNTAIN

"Yeah. I'm flying out Wednesday. My college buddy, Dennis, is coming home, too. We're a committee of two on class reunion plans for next year. We could have done it by phone, but it gives me the chance to see my favorite girl¾you."

Caron could not contain her excitement. "Fantastic. It'll be so good to see you. I've missed my friend. Have you got someone to pick you up at the airport?"

"All taken care of. Dennis is flying in the same day. We've got a rental car to drive on up to North Fork."

"So where are you staying?"

"With Dennis. We'll be at his parent's house. I'll call and we'll set a time to get together. I want to catch up on everything. Are you still with Bill?"

"Yes. We're on our way into town to check security tapes at feed stores. I'll bring you up-to-date on everything that's happened since we last talked. I'm staying at Bill's farm. The only time I go to the apartment is to get more clothes."

"I want to know about it all. I'll call you when I get settled and we'll make plans for dinner and a long visit. I want to meet this Bill who rooted me out as your favorite guy."

"Meeting Bill has been the best part of the move to North Fork." She was relieved to see Bill's mouth lift in a half smile when she slipped a sideways peek. Her intuition had warned her there might be a tad of jealousy. But she also had mixed feelings about his deceased wife.

"I'll call when I get settled."

"How long will you be staying?"

"I haven't decided. I've got a week's vacation and some accumulated sick days. You know the company policy¾use them or lose them."

"Well, let me know when you get in town. I'm so looking forward to seeing you."

"Ditto, girlfriend. See you soon."

Caron could not prevent the deep sigh that escaped when she ended the call. She sat back farther into the seat, pleased Bruce was coming to visit. Pleasant millisecond scenes skittered through her brain. For a moment she experienced sadness for her old stomping grounds and what she had to give up because of the stalker.

"Are you okay?" Bill's arm stretched across the empty space to rest on the back of her neck.

"I'm fine. Had a Los Angeles flashback for a moment."

"Do you miss it?"

"There are aspects I enjoyed, but North Fork also has its advantages." This time it was her arm that reached across to nudge Bill on the shoulder. Her reward was a wide grin as they pulled into the City Diner parking lot.

Nothing else was said until they got inside the diner and chose a booth.

"When will your Bruce arrive in North Fork?"

"My Bruce?" She could not stop the giggle that bubbled into her throat. "He said Wednesday. He's meeting his friend Dennis, son of the publisher who got me the job here. They're planning a class reunion. And he's not *my* Bruce, but a friend. He'll be staying with Dennis, but he wants to have dinner with us and catch up."

"With us?"

"Both of us. I want you to meet him. More importantly, I want Bruce to meet you, the man who has taken on my problem, the person I care for and the one who has kept me safe."

"I'll make a confession. I was a little jealous about the relationship you have with Bruce, but then realized I have a past, too." She responded to his sheepish grin with her own smile. Bill reached across the table to cover her hand with his. "I'm looking forward to meeting him."

They made quick work of the diner's Saturday morning

breakfast special and were back in Truck driving to their first stop. Caron walked beside him into the store.

"Jimmy. How we doing? It's good to see you," Bill said, walking up to the counter and shaking the employee's hand.

"Hey, Bill. Where you been hiding? It's been a while."

"Yes, it has. Gotta problem and need your help. By the way, this is Caron Kimble."

"Read some of your articles. Nice to meet you." He turned to another employee. "Larry, take over for me," he said and stepped from behind the counter.

He stopped in front of Bill. "What's up?"

"Do you remember any stranger who has been in recently to purchase a pesticide?"

Jimmy tilted his head to the side and lowered it a bit. There was no immediate response as he appeared to consider the question. He leaned against the counter and propped an elbow on its surface before looking directly at Bill. "Don't remember anyone offhand."

"Have you got security cameras?"

"Two¾one for the counter area and the other for the parking lot. Whatcha need?"

"How long do you keep the tapes?"

"They get erased every forty-eight hours and we reuse them. What's up?"

"I'm looking for the last two weeks or maybe longer."

"If you need to go back that far there's only one store that might still have them¾Chandler's Farm Supply. They keep them for about a month. I know because I have a friend that works in the office over there."

"Chandler's. That's what I need to know. Jimmy, you're a big help¾always have been. I don't really know the folks that well at Chandler's. Who do I need to see?"

"Ask for Shelia. She works in the office where all the monitors are installed. Tell her I sent you over."

"Thanks, Jimmy. I owe you one."

"Can I ask what you're looking for?"

"Someone put pesticide into hamburger meat and tossed it out for Token."

"She survive?"

"Yes. I'm looking for any unfamiliar face that might have purchased pesticides lately."

"Hope you get the scum bucket."

"We'll head on over to Chandler's. If we have time I'll come back and take a look at the guns."

"We'll be here 'til five," Jimmy said.

Bill turned to Caron. "Chandler's is a couple of miles out of the city limits. Maybe they'll have something on video."

This farm supply was bigger than the first one on their list. When they pulled into the parking lot, Caron noticed raised platforms on the side and men loading sacks of feed onto waiting pickups.

"Looks like they have quite an operation here," Caron said.

"I keep going to Jimmy when I need something. He's always given me good advice on products. I don't know these folks but they have a good reputation."

Bill went straight to the counter when they got inside, showed his identification and asked to see Shelia. They were shuffled to an office where a woman was seated at a desk. She glanced up from her work when they walked into the room.

"Shelia?" Bill said.

"Yes."

"Jimmy sent us over. I'm Bill Bonner." He showed her his identification and introduced Caron.

"How can I help you?"

Bill explained what he was looking for ¾ wanted to see security tapes and ask employees if they noticed any unfamiliar person buying pesticides in a small quantity within the last month. "Most producers buy pesticides in bulk," he said. Nothing was included about the stalker.

"We keep tapes for a month. You're welcome to take a look. I'll set you up a place in the corner and you can take your time. There's several disks."

Shelia gave Bill a quick lesson on how to operate the system and returned to her work. Caron moved a chair next to him. They started the search.

After two hours Caron had observed nothing familiar¾ordinary business scenes with customers who paid at the counter and out the door. She stood to give her back a rest and stretch her arms. It was nearing the lunch hour. Bill tapped the pause button.

"Mr. Bonner, some employees have lunch in the break room. It might be a good time to ask them any questions," Shelia said.

"Thanks. Caron, why don't you take a break while I go talk to them," Bill said. He rose to exit the office.

"Caron, there's a soda machine in the break room," Shelia said.

As they walked Bill put a hand at the small of her back and massaged the muscles a bit.

When they reached the break area, Bill headed toward the employees. Caron got a drink and went back to Shelia's office. She sat down in front of the monitor and tapped the key to take the system off pause.

She had almost finished the drink. Bill had not returned. Shelia was focused on the ledgers spread across her desk. Caron continued to watch the monitor.

As she turned up the plastic soda container to drain the last of her drink, her eyes locked on the image of a man who had made his way up to the counter. Caron's hand froze. Her body straightened and went rigid. The ball cap was so low over the forehead she could not see the face but memories burned through her brain. The compressed air she held in her lungs released in a deep whoosh when she jumped up too fast. *It's him¾ the cap.*

For a moment Caron's legs stayed rooted to the tile floor. Sporadic images of her life since she left Los Angeles blipped through her mind. *You miserable piece of garbage. Gotcha!* She sped to the door and never made it through the opening, but ran right into Bill.

"Whoa," he said, catching and holding her at arm's length.

Tears smarted her eyes.

"What is it?" he said.

Caron took a swipe at her wet cheeks, irritated the discovery made her emotional. "I found him."

Bill's expression changed to deathly calm. "Show me." He took her arm and nudged her back to the monitor. The disk had to be reversed. Shelia watched from her desk.

"There. I recognize the hat and he's the size I remember."

Bill stared at the monitor. They watched as the man made his purchase. The product was clearly visible. It was a pesticide.

"You son of a…" He did not finish the sentence, but turned to Shelia who had been watching.

"Shelia, I'm going to need to borrow this disk."

"As long as you return it when you do what you gotta do."

While Shelia was talking, Bill opened his flip phone and scrolled down its contact list. His attention was fixed on Caron when he tapped a number and spoke. "Wallace, we got a body."

CHAPTER 22

Caron was convinced she had entered time warp speed having to concentrate on quicker and longer steps to keep up with Bill. His face was as hard as flint. A firm hand cupped her elbow as they headed to Truck.

"Wallace will meet us at the station. We'll take a closer look at the disk and maybe he can run a hard copy photo today." Backing Truck from the parking space, his heavy foot on the accelerator caused a squeal of tires. He stopped and glanced at Carol. "I guess if I have to enforce speed limits I need to observe them, too." He eased up on the gas pedal, but the tension in the hands gripping the steering wheel remained steadfast.

Wallace was getting out of his car just as they pulled into the parking lot.

Bill grabbed the disk he had laid on the seat between them. "Come on."

She pulled up the passenger door handle and swirled her body so both feet hit the cement at the same time, and made it around the front of Truck and beside Bill in record time.

"What we got?" Wallace said as Bill handed him the tape.

"Caron identified the cap he's wearing, the same one he had on when all this started in Los Angeles. The frame needs to be enlarged to see if we can get more detail." There was no pause in the conversation.

"We'll take a look. Is there anything else you can remember, Caron?" Wallace said.

"His height and size are the same as I saw on the disk. I remember when I bumped into him I didn't have to look up too much to apologize and I'm five-five. I just know that's the same cap. I remember the initials SUCS."

They walked down a hall and into another room. Caron took one step back, astonished at the display of video equipment that took up three walls of space. Wallace sat down at a monitor and inserted the disk into the desktop computer.

"I was watching the video while Bill was asking the employees at Chandler's questions," she said.

Wallace worked the computer keyboard and Caron focused. Bill remained silent. The only sound in the room was the constant hum of the machine that held the disk.

"There." Caron's voice rose. She pointed at the monitor. "That's him."

Wallace stopped the disk and backed it up. Three pairs of eyes stared. The man kept his head at a low angle but the SUCS initials were clearly visible. He placed his purchase, a small bag of pesticide, on the counter. The employee rang up the sale. Caron's nightmare then turned and left the building. He kept his head down but she could see the side of his face.

"Can I get copies? We'll go back to Chandler's and I'll show them to the employees¾ see if we can get more description," Bill said.

"I'll send out copies today to area motels. He's got to be holed up someplace. Bill, you know what we got here is only circumstantial. How many of these hats exist and, Caron, you said you don't remember enough about his face to make a positive ID?"

"At least we've got a little more to work with," Bill said. He took the photocopies Wallace handed him. "I'll let you know what we find out. Man, I know you're going an extra mile and I appreciate it. This is your day off, too. Caron's not safe as long as this maniac is out there and I owe him one for hurting Token."

"That was just mean. You got my number. Let me know what you find out. I'm going to make the rounds at motels in the city." Wallace began to print out more pictures as Bill and Caron left the room. "Stay in touch," he said.

Caron stopped when Bill paused in the hallway. He stared at the pictures and rolled them into a long cylinder. "We'll get him, Caron. We've got to hurry back to Chandler's before they close."

Employees were moving display merchandise from the outside front area into the building when they pulled up in the parking lot. Bill had not released the pictures from his grip.

They hurried inside.

Shelia was standing at the counter when they went in. "You're back," she said.

"We'll return the disk. I'll see to that personally. They're printing photos. I wanted ya'll to take a look at these and see if there's anything you can remember about this man." Bill unrolled the pictures and flattened them on the counter with both hands.

"Come and take a look, fellows." Shelia motioned for the counter employees to come closer. They gathered around her. There were no customers in the store since it was so close to closing. They looked at the pictures and disappointment started to grow when Caron saw the negative shake of their heads.

"Take a close look. This is very important," Bill said.

The employees shuffled and looked at the photos again. But nothing changed.

A voice piped in from another aisle. "What's going on?" An employee approached the counter and the other men made a path for him.

"Take a look at these pictures, Monk. Do you remember seeing this dude?" Shelia asked.

The picture was pushed along the counter to Monk. He leaned forward and propped an elbow on the laminate surface and stared. A wide grin pressed his full lips into a straight line and his eyes lit up. "Sure do. I remember the cap. Thought the initials were kind of unusual¾said he needed a pesticide for roses¾stopped by here because he couldn't get back home before the place where he does business closed."

"Can you describe him?" Bill said.

"Well, yeah. He would not look directly at me and sort of mumbled when he talked."

"Did he say where he lived or did his regular business?"

"I didn't ask. Sorry."

Bill flipped the picture over on the blank side and grabbed a pen from a box on the counter. "Anything you could remember would help."

"Well, I'd guess his height around five-seven or -eight. I could tell his hair was dark brown from the sideburns. He had a light complexion, actually kinda pale."

"What about his eyes?" Bill said. He pushed the photo closer to the employee. "How about nose? Mouth?"

"Don't remember the eyes, but there *was* a mole over the left eyebrow. Well, it was smack dab in the middle of the eyebrow," Monk said.

Caron's body responded to the words she heard. A flash of heat rippled its way to her face. She could feel the flush, took a deep breath, and continued to listen.

"He was on the slim size, maybe hundred-fifty pounds. Someone new coming in the store, you know, sticks out like a sore thumb. That's about all I do remember."

"That's a big help." Bill handed the employee a card. "If you remember anything else¾anything at all—you have my number. Call anytime, day or night."

As soon as they got outside, Bill pulled the cell phone from his pocket, flipped it open, and tapped a number. "Wallace, we got more ID."

Caron listened to Bill relay what they had discovered.

"Wallace is already getting the photos out to the motels. Jimmy's place will be closed by the time we get there. We'll check out his gun inventory Monday. Wallace is making rounds to the motels."

"I'm still not comfortable with this gun thing."

"We could postpone it since we have more identification."

"That suits me fine," she said as they got into Truck.

"I sure would like to go to church tomorrow, but I need to stop by the apartment for a dress."

When they pulled into the parking lot, Bill said, "Wait. I'll get the door." She did as he requested, aware of a crisp edge in his voice.

He opened the door to the foyer and stepped aside for Caron to enter first then moved on to the apartment entrance. Bill came to an abrupt stop, stared at the metal knob to her partially opened apartment door. When she felt his body tense and a protective arm reach out to block her progress, she froze. He settled in front of her. She put a hand against the wall for support.

"Stay here," he said, leaned over and removed a small gun hidden under his pants leg.

She did as he said, her body transformed to match his tense and alert state.

He took up a position and pushed lightly against the door

with a booted foot. It swung open without a sound. A quick move, gun held upright in his right hand, and he disappeared inside. Caron inhaled a deep breath and listened.

She whispered his name. "Bill?"

Relief surged through her body when he stepped back into the foyer.

"Be prepared. It's a mess."

He stayed in front of her. She was prepared to face disarray but not ready for the scene that was her living room.

"Oh! ... Bill."

"Don't touch anything." He flipped open his phone and tapped.

Caron walked deeper into the living room area.

She heard "Wallace" but her focus was on the shreds of upholstering stuffing that were scattered on the floor. Long, savage cuts had been made in the recliner and sofa and the foam rubber pulled out. As she tiptoed around the scattered pieces, a dread to see what waited for her in the bedroom slowed her footsteps.

Dresser drawers were emptied and the doors to her closet stood opened. Disbelief raged through her mind when she summoned the courage to look inside. Pieces of shredded clothing hung limp from the hangers, the remainder in haphazard piles on the floor. Tears smarted her eyes. Bill stood behind her, talking to Wallace.

"Yeah. It's pretty bad. Okay. We'll see you shortly."

He closed the phone and put his arms around her. She leaned back against his chest and sobbed.

"Wallace is on his way. Caron, things can be replaced. I'm thankful you weren't here." His embrace tightened. "This is rage¾anger."

He nudged her back to the living room and that's where they were standing, Bill's arms around her, when Wallace came through the apartment door.

"Looks like someone was pretty mad and took it out on the furniture," he said, taking a scan of the living room and walking toward the bedroom.

"Are you thinking what I'm thinking?" Wallace addressed Bill with the question. "The TV set wasn't taken."

"This was not theft. It was pure rage," Bill said.

"Can you tell if anything is missing?"

"We haven't touched anything. Called you first," Bill said.

"Caron, take a walk through and see if you can determine if anything has been taken."

"Just a mess in the living room. It looks like whoever it was didn't bother to go in the kitchen." She went into the bedroom.

The contents of her jewelry box had been dumped onto the dresser, but it didn't look as if anything was missing. Her extra makeup containers were on the floor. It was as if someone made one long swipe to push everything off the dresser top. The only way she would be able to determine if anything had been taken was to pick it all up and put it back in its proper place. Bill remained close.

"Wallace, I just can't tell. It's all such a mess. I didn't have that much jewelry. But it looks like it's all there, just scattered. My clothes are ruined."

"Caron, you don't need to be in this apartment. She needs to continue staying at your place, Bill. What's this?"

Wallace was standing beside her bed. He picked up a scrap of paper partially hidden under the pillow. His attention first went to the paper and then a quick look to Bill before handing it over to him. "I'd say this confirms it was no theft, but the intruder was most likely Caron's stalker."

Bill was only one step away. His eyes were locked on the scrap of paper. He reached out and pulled her close.

"I want to see," she said.

Bill hesitated, first looking at Wallace then back to the

scrap of paper before he placed it in Caron's outstretched hand.

Only two words were scrawled across the small piece of paper.

"You're next."

She started to shake.

CHAPTER 23

Caron lost control over the mental images that seared a hot path of reality through her mind and pushed her into the depth of depression. The destruction in her apartment was the act of an individual whose aim had meant to ravage and terrify. She wanted the fear to end, be cut away and removed from her life. If it had not been for Bill she would have drowned in a pool of despair. He had literally saved her emotional and physical life.

The haunting words on the scrap of paper honed her nerves to razor edge. She had knee-jerk reactions from any unexpected sound or touch and apologized more than once to Jennifer and Vicki. Bill shared everything he and Wallace discussed. Absorbing a stream of new information became the norm. Her sole comfort was being at the farm with Bill and Token. She had no desire to return to the apartment. Going to the farm after work became a natural part of ending the day. At night she was content to lay in the peaceful embrace of Bill's arms and escape the horror in the outside world. A pause in intimacy was in silent agreement.

"How did your day go?" Bill asked as they walked toward her car in the parking lot on Wednesday.

"Boring," she said. "Vicki went with me to the department store to pick up a few items, enough to get me by for a couple of days. That is the only time I've been out. Having to stay in the office and others doing my assignments is getting on my nerves."

"Maybe it won't be much longer."

"I feel so guilty with Jennifer and Vicki doing their work and mine, too. Is there anything new?"

"We know this maniac isn't staying at any of the local motels. Wallace checked each one and sent info to adjoining areas. We'll get him. Have you heard from Bruce?"

"This morning. He and Dennis are getting settled at Mr. Wilson's place. We'll meet for lunch at the diner tomorrow, then dinner Friday. Can you meet us at the diner?"

He stretched out an arm, rested his hand on the back of her neck and caressed the skin. "You can plan on it. The only time I want you out of my sight is when you're sitting in the office," he said.

"I'll be at the church tomorrow evening to help put up Christmas decorations in the sanctuary. Remember, Reverend Jon mentioned it Sunday during the sermon."

"I'll follow you to the church, then go on to a district meeting at the courthouse. We have one every month or so. I'll join you as soon as the meeting is over."

As they pulled into the driveway, Caron saw Bill flip open his phone. When they parked he continued talking to the caller. She got her purse and made her way around Truck. When Bill got out the expression on his face was so revealing she responded with a quick laugh.

He swooped her up off the ground in a tight hug and whirled her around.

"That phone call must be good news. Did you win the lottery?"

"Better than that. We got a great lead from a motel over in Russellville. The identification Wallace faxed fits a man who *was* staying there. He's going over to look at security tapes, see if anything shows up on a vehicle."

Bill had not released her. It was the moment to rise above the emotional trauma and feel exhilaration. Her arms wound around his neck and she laughed out loud between kisses planted on his neck, chin, and cheeks. He began to lower her very slowly. The hard muscles of his body and his intense stare at her lips ignited a fire that had smoldered for days. She melted against him and would not loosen her embrace that left her on tiptoes. The smile on his face changed to a mischievous grin and a devilish glint flamed in his eyes.

"Don't stop. That's nice." He pulled her closer and wrapped his arms around her. The pause from intimacy was over. It was time to celebrate. His arms tightened.

* * *

CARON GLANCED into the rearview mirror. Bill was a couple of car lengths behind her. The euphoria from a night of making love remained strong. She could still feel his hot skin pushing and lifting her to new heights of ecstasy. There was no need to turn on temperature control when she remembered the heat that was generated between them. The late November sun penetrated the front windshield and added to her warmth. She lowered the side window for a breath of cooling air on her face.

She was comfortable with their relationship. It seemed natural from the time they met. *I think it was fate.* No four-letter word had been spoken, but Bill had become her friend, protector, and lover. The aura of comfort that surrounded her when they were together was peaceful and calm. The only good that came out of her emotional battle and flight from the stalker was meeting Bill. She acknowledged to herself the future was yet to be written.

As they pulled into the diner's lot, Bruce was getting out of a vehicle. She parked alongside of the car, jumped out, and hurried to where he stood. He slid his arms around her. Bill moved up to stand closer.

"You're a sight for sore eyes, girl. I can't believe I'm here. This has got to be Bill."

He released Caron and stepped forward to extend a hand to Bill.

"Good to finally meet you, Bruce. Caron has spoken very highly of you. And I want to thank you for keeping her protected until I could take over."

Caron sighed a breath of relief, thankful it was not an awkward meeting between the two men, one a friend, the other her lover.

"I'm glad she has you. Caron has been a best friend, like a little sister, forever. It was a long path of troubling events even before she moved from Los Angeles. I never dreamed this maniac would follow her across the country."

They settled Caron between them and continued to talk on their way into the diner.

Bill nudged Caron into the seat and slid in beside her.

"I see your taste for hot dogs hasn't changed," Bruce said and laughed at her order, then turned his attention to Bill.

"My blood turned to ice water when my apartment was broken into," Bruce said. "I had this weird feeling when I saw my desk ransacked. The investigating officers said it appeared the intruder was looking for something. I had to get a new lock for the front door that had been jimmied open. I told them about Caron's stalker and what had happened in the past. It never crossed my mind he would follow her from Los Angeles to North Fork. Bring me up-to-date."

Caron added little as Bill related what had happened since she arrived in North Fork and Bruce asked questions. When there was a break, she said, "Bruce, I don't know what I would have done if not for Bill. He's been my emotional rock since the night of the farm banquet when the stalker called. It was so hard for me to even comprehend this man followed me to North Fork." She looked at Bill and wanted to reach over and kiss him soundly when she saw his mellow gaze focused on her.

"You are going to continue staying at Bill's place until this situation is resolved?" Bruce asked.

"She'll stay with me where I can keep her safe," Bill said.

Caron did not miss the grin that twitched on Bruce's lips, and then the open smile that followed.

"Appears you have it all under control. Do I see something permanent in the future that's going to require me making another visit to North Fork?" He chuckled.

There was no stopping the spastic jerk of her head, a sideways glance at Bill, and a millisecond interpretation of his facial expression. It was a look of total surprise. She forced her attention back on Bruce and waded in to a flurry of words.

"We've just become good friends," she said.

Bill said nothing. The silence loomed and she thought it would never end. *Why doesn't he say something?*

As if he heard her plea, a big hand covered hers and squeezed. She was so relieved. Bill turned to face her directly. "There's time to talk about us later, but first we need to get this fanatic off her back and out of the picture. She stays with me."

When she saw the set of his jaw and lips, a pleasant sensation started its run from head to toe, curled and waited to share in the happy moment. She pressed her hip against his. All she wanted to do was snuggle and absorb his strength. Bill's phone started to hum. Caron straightened her position in the booth and focused her attention on Bruce, who was leaning back against the vinyl cushioning and beaming like a Cheshire cat.

Bill answered the phone. Caron could feel the muscles in his body tense.

"Wallace. What's up?"

She felt him go rigid and alert. The mellow countenance on his face changed to a mask of silent, stone-solid concentration.

"You're sure? That's the break we've needed." Bill pulled a small notepad from the upper pocket of his uniform shirt. "What's the make, model, color, and is there any other identifiable markings on the vehicle?" He went silent, listened, and wrote on a blank sheet in the pad. "Anything else?" He leaned forward as he listened to Wallace.

"Keep in touch. I'll be looking for the vehicle, too. You've got the city covered." He ended the conversation and leaned against Caron.

"They have a picture of this dude getting into a vehicle. It's a rental. They got the company name. The outside security camera at the motel recorded him." Bill's eyes glittered. He had transitioned into a state trooper ready to pursue a criminal. "I need to get back on the highway with this information. Let's get you back to the newspaper office."

"What can I do?" Bruce asked.

Bill looked across the table at Bruce and then to her. He looked down at the table surface. She saw the hesitation, a pause, but then he aimed his attention on Bruce. His voice was firm and spoken at a fast clip.

"The sooner I get back on the highway, the more time I'll have to search for this nerd. Will you follow Caron back to her office? And, Caron, under no circumstances do you go out of the building for the rest of the day. I'll be there to meet you when you get off and follow you to the church, go to my meeting, and follow you back to the farm."

"Go. You can be sure I'll get her back to the office and walk her inside."

The decision was made. Caron slid out of the booth. Bill's wide leather belt squeaked from its rub against the seat vinyl as he moved swiftly to get up and stand toe-to-toe with her.

"I'll see you this afternoon." He made a quick step away from her, then came to an abrupt stop, faced her fully, put his hands on her shoulders, and gave her a playful shake. His lips pressed against hers in a firm kiss and then he hurried toward the exit door.

"I'd say there's no doubt about his feelings," Bruce said.

She smiled, responding to his amused grin. "You will always be my friend. Lord knows you've put up with me for so long. I cherish your friendship. Bill¾he's become so important to me in such a short time. He's the fairy-tale prince in this nightmare."

"Caron, I thought you would be tucked away and safe when I suggested you move here. To follow you all the way across country, this guy has got to be mentally unbalanced and that's dangerous."

"Tell me about it. I have heard stories about that happening to other people, but I never dreamed just how traumatic it could be. Let's change the subject. Is there anyone new in your life?"

"Not to speak of. You know me¾sun and fun. Not ready to get serious."

There was not enough time to say all that was needed to be said since the clock on the wall became a reminder that she needed to get back to the office.

"We'll have the whole evening to talk at dinner," she said.

Bruce followed her through town, not getting over a car length behind her vehicle. He reminded her again to follow Bill's instructions and not leave the office. She gave him a quick hug at the front of the building and he stood there until she had opened the door and stepped inside.

Jennifer and Vicki had returned from lunch and were out on appointments. That left her to face a tiresome afternoon. Trying to make herself useful and file copy required too much of an effort. It was at least an hour to go before Bill would arrive to escort her to church. She took a deep breath and parked in front of the computer, pulled up past issues, and read to pass the time.

When the door opened and Bill's frame filled the entrance she was ready to jump out of her skin to get rid of the boredom. She got out of the chair and didn't stop until she was across the room and throwing her arms around him for a tight squeeze.

"Well, I think I'll go out and come back in again. I like that kind of welcome." It was no small grin he had on his face. It was a full-fledged smile of appreciation.

"I'm so glad to see you. This afternoon has been such a drudge. Let's get out of here."

She hurried ahead of Bill down the hall and descended the steps. Outside the front door she lifted her head skyward and inhaled a deep breath. "Oh, the fresh air is so good."

Bill reached for her hand. "So, you had a boring afternoon?"

"Totally. How was your day? Did you find out anything more?"

"Nothing more than what you already know. He'll show up. There's an APB out here and in surrounding counties. Wallace confirmed the car rental information. It's just a matter of time before he makes a wrong move." He gave her hand a reassuring squeeze. "We'll concentrate on keeping you safe."

She returned the gesture. "Don't take this wrong. I love being with you, but I am looking forward to working with the group tonight at the church. It's been such a boring afternoon."

It was only four blocks to the church and Bill was on her tail every foot of the way. Several vehicles were already in the parking lot when they arrived. She sat and waited for him to reach the passenger's side of her vehicle before getting out. He walked her to the entrance.

"I'll be back right after the meeting. It shouldn't take long¾just routine."

"With all of us working together it won't take that long. I'll stay here," she said.

"And stay inside," he said. "What's going on over there?" Bill was watching several children with an adult go into an adjacent building.

Caron studied the group. "Oh, some of those kids belong to the folks who are putting up decorations in the church. They may have decided to do their classrooms while their parents were doing the sanctuary."

Bill turned his attention back to Caron. He moved close and put his hands on her elbows, slid them up to float across her shoulders and cup her chin. The sensation gave her pleasure.

"That's nice," she said.

"One more thing," he said and lifted her chin so he could look into her eyes. "About what Bruce said at lunchtime. I do want us to talk about a lot of things when this situation gets settled, among them the immediate future."

She cocked her head to the side and felt playful. "Is that a threat or a promise?"

"You can take that to the bank. It's a promise," he said and dipped his head to plant a quick kiss on her lips.

"I'll make sure that note accrues interest," she said.

"I'll be back in no time. Now get inside¾I'll wait."

He opened the door and she stepped inside, still delighting in the kiss. She took her time walking to the sanctuary where she could hear voices. "Hey, Caron. Just in time to give me a hand with this trim on the balcony." Regina stood in the aisle, her arms filled with greenery.

The men were setting up Christmas trees adjacent to the altar area. Regina and Caron started for the steps to the balcony.

"Oh no. Regina, I forgot my phone. Let me run back and get it. It's on the car seat. Give me just a sec. I'll meet you in the balcony."

Caron turned and hurried from the sanctuary, down the hall, and through the exit door to the parking lot. The sun was gone for the day. A cooler breeze played with the tree branches. She ignored the black shadows around the cedars and started to her car, knowing she was going against Bill's orders, but her phone was a necessity. It would cause him more worry if he called and she did not answer. Mentally, she complained about the time change that made it get dark an hour earlier.

Her eyes lifted to search for the owners of young voices she heard clamoring in playful tones. A couple of the kids were walking across the parking lot totally involved in conversation. Their chatter continued even when they reached a vehicle and opened the front door.

Caron was only a few feet from her car when a sweaty hand covered her mouth and an arm reached around her. She was jammed against a body from behind in a split second.

"One word and it will be your last, my love."

ECHOES FROM THE MOUNTAIN

Caron felt cold metal press against the side of her throat.

The voice rasped against her ear lobe. "Don't call or do anything or I'll hurt those kids over there. It's up to you."

She remained silent.

She could make out images of the kids in the interior light of the vehicle. "There it is. That's what she wanted," Caron heard one of the boys say. "Come on. Let's get back inside. Mrs. Milligan is waiting for these scissors."

Caron's eyes smarted. She knew she was in trouble, but could not endanger anyone else. Her lips wanted to scream for help, but she remained silent.

"Good, my love. Not a word. We're going for a little ride."

CHAPTER 24

Bill was anxious. The district captain was late for the meeting and that kicked his fidget button into high gear. When he did arrive, their first topic to discuss was data relayed to his office by Wallace on the suspected stalker.

"Ya'll have the info. We're going to join other law enforcement agencies in the surrounding area and give this extra attention. He's after Bill's girlfriend." He paused and nodded in Bill's direction. "I hope you don't mind me telling that, Bill. I talked to Wallace about another matter and he told me. We want this piece of trash behind bars."

"Thanks, Captain," Bill said. "His name is Dexter Fench and he was staying in a motel over in Russellville. Investigators got a call after the information went out. He was identified in their security tapes and so was the vehicle. We got the rental company name. New info has him in a black van. We have the make and model. Wallace Thompson has the lead on this case and he's already sent out the description."

"There you have it. Watch for this man. He needs to be put away," the captain said.

One by one the agenda items were discussed. The

meeting was running longer than Bill expected. They opted for a short break. As he walked from the room into the hall he tapped in Caron's number on his cell phone. He waited for the connecting ring. It rang. No answer. It hummed again and connected to her voice mail.

He consoled himself as he listened to her message and contemplated she may not have been in a position to answer.

"Hey, Caron. I probably caught you at a bad time, but when you have time, call me."

He ended the call and walked down the hall to a water fountain. A picture of her, arms filled with Christmas decorations and unable to answer a ringing phone, filled his mind. He wanted to talk with her, let her know he was running late and to stay inside the building until he arrived. Surely the meeting wouldn't go much longer. There were only a couple of other procedural items to be addressed.

He pressed her number again. The phone rang. No answer. His mind again reasoned her failure to answer was just a moment when she could not get to the phone, but a nagging doubt crept into his thoughts. Knowing she was inside with people was no comfort, and there was no preventing the growing ominous feeling that sprouted in his stomach. Now he was thankful Caron had insisted he add Bruce's telephone number to his contacts in case they needed to communicate about Friday night dinner plans. He scrolled down the list and tapped dial. Bruce answered on the third ring.

"Bruce. Bill Bonner. Need a favor."

"What's up?"

"My meeting is running long and I'm suppose to meet Caron at St. Luther's Church. She's there with a group putting up Christmas decorations. Would you go stay with her until I can get there?"

"No problem."

"This meeting shouldn't take much longer. Caron didn't know how long the job at the church would take either, but if they get finished and lock up she doesn't need to be outside alone."

"I'm walking out the door as we're talking."

"I'd feel better under the circumstances. She doesn't need to be alone. I don't think there's a problem, but want someone there for her."

"I got this covered. Dennis went to pick up his dad. Plenty of time before Mrs. Wilson's dinner tonight."

"Thanks, Bruce. I'll see you at the church. Call me when you get there."

"Got it."

Bill welcomed the warm flush of relief when he ended the call. He credited the persistent niggling in his chest as being overly protective. Everything was under control. Before he went back into the conference room he tried to call her again. The call went to voicemail. He begrudged the tormenting minutes. When the meeting finally concluded, he made a quick round of handshaking and was out the door. His long strides covered the distance to the patrol car in seconds. Wanting to get to the church was all that was on his mind.

He stopped for the traffic light at the corner of the church parking lot. His left foot held firm on the brake pedal but the right one made nervous taps on the accelerator. When he eased forward, closer to the pedestrian lane, he observed a group standing around a parked car. His cell phone rang.

"Hello."

"Bill. Bruce. Where are you?"

"At the corner."

"Hurry."

Bill's blood turned to ice water. Unstoppable chill bumps scrambled up his spine. "Where are you? I see a group."

"I'm with them."

Bill goosed the speed, turned right on red, and pulled into the parking lot. Bruce made a dead run toward the patrol car.

"What?" Bill slung the door open and addressed Bruce before he even got out. He held his breath for Bruce's answer.

"Caron's not here."

Bill's body temperature dropped another ten degrees. "What do you mean, she's not here?" His heart rate increased to jackhammer speed. The group had moved closer to him.

"This lady, Regina, said Caron left her phone in the car and went to get it. When she didn't come back, they went to check on her. They searched the building after they found Caron's phone on the front car seat. That's when I got here."

Bill directed his attention to Regina. "She didn't say anything else when she said she was going to get her phone."

"No, just that she had to get it. Said she wouldn't be gone but a second. I was holding a pretty big string of trim so I waited. I got concerned when she didn't come back. It should have taken no time at all to get the phone."

Bruce handed Bill Caron's phone. The security light from the overhead utility pole did not hide the flushed skin on Bruce's face. "Here's her phone," he said.

"I have Caron's purse," Regina said.

Bill stood very still, every muscle in a state of cocked and ready. His fists clenched and unclenched. His attention was dead set on the shadows outside the lit parking lot and in a blink focused on the building. "Is that a security camera?"

One man in the group spoke up. "Yes, officer. With these incidents in other churches we had security cameras installed. Especially here on the street side of the church." The man identified himself as Wesley Sears.

"Where's the monitor."

"In the church office. I don't have a key."

"Who has?"

"Patsy, the church secretary."

"Call her," Bill said.

Wesley pulled a phone from his pocket and tapped in a number.

Bill lifted his phone from the front shirt pocket and flipped it open.

"Man, I'm sorry," Bruce said. "What can I do?"

Bill lifted a hand to indicate a "hold on" mode and spoke into the phone.

"Wallace, Bill. I'm at St. Luther's Church. Caron was with a group decorating this evening. She left her phone in the car, said she was going to get it but didn't return. Yeah¾I'm not going anywhere."

"I should have got here earlier. Man, you don't think…?"

"Don't even go there," Bill said. "The important thing is to find Caron."

"I'll do whatever you want."

Bill turned and spoke to Wesley. "Where's the secretary?"

"On her way. There she is now." A van swung into the upper side of the parking lot. The driver got out and waved, made a motion for them to meet her at the front of the church.

BILL AND BRUCE headed in that direction. As they approached her, Bill heard the squealing tires of a vehicle. It was Wallace. The car pulled into the parking lot and stopped a couple of feet away. The door popped open and he leaped from the vehicle, did not stop until he stood beside Bill. "What we got?" he asked Bill.

"We're going to the church office to check the security monitor." Nothing else was said as the men hustled toward the building.

Patsy had the office open and was waiting when they entered the side door. She was standing in front of the monitor. "Reverse the tape slowly," Bill said, and stopped in front of the monitor.

All eyes first centered on Patsy and then the monitor as her fingers moved across letters on the keyboard. Blurred images skittered across the screen. They found what they wanted.

"There," Bill said. "Pause the tape and move it forward slowly." Their concentration was fixed on the monitor.

Bill watched, his face a mask of stone as Caron walked from the church building toward her car. She walked fast, unaware of the man who made a quick exit from a van and almost ran at her from the side. They watched mesmerized, saw the glint of a knife pulled from the man's pocket and snapped open. Bill's breath stopped in his throat. He wanted to shout a warning. *Stop! It's him.*

Their eyes did not flinch from watching as the stalker's arm went around Caron and pulled her backward. It appeared he was saying something against Caron's ear, but the security light was dimmer where they stood. Bill's arms, straight as a board on each side, ended in clenched fists.

Wallace took a step forward. His hand rested on the counter where the monitor sat. He leaned closer to peer at the screen. "It's our suspect," he said. His eyes were flinty.

Bill's hand jerked as he rose and gripped the butt of his gun. He wanted to hurt the man who held Caron, but could only stand and watch. There could be no rescue from what had already happened.

He could not stop the mental images that crowded his mind for a split second, long enough for him to remember emotional rage and the helpless feeling that resurrected itself from the past.

Scenes from memory injected a new fear¾one he remembered but cursed as it raised its ugly head. Caron's life was in danger. The same way Katherine's had been when she and Pat were running from the monster who hunted them on the West Virginia mountain. He and his friend, Allen, armed themselves with high-powered rifles and went into the mountains to find the women they loved.

Bill faced Wallace.

"He's got her."

CHAPTER 25

Dexter was so giddy his fingers drummed the steering wheel in a broken rhythm to the tune he attempted to hum. He was convinced fate had intervened and delivered her to him. His body throbbed for relief. *Got to wait. Wait. Wait. Got to wait. There'll be plenty of time, but first I'm going to give her a taste of the torment she sent me through. When that trooper finds her, there'll be nothing left for him.*

He had watched from the shopping center parking lot across from the diner when they got out of the vehicles and positioned Caron between them. It had been a matter of persistence to learn Caron's routine. That state trooper was around her all the time. Dexter had followed and kept a safe distance. He checked out of the motel and turned in the rental sedan for a van. There had been some anxious moments about the possibility of discovery before he could finish his "little project" so he decided not to get another motel room and sleep in the van.

The anger burned every time he saw Caron with the trooper. The four flat tires and feeding that dog a little treat didn't help. He was ready to give her another warning, knew when she got off from work, so waited down the block in the van. It was a simple matter to follow them to that trooper's house. He would wait until late night, slip into the driveway, and key the side of her car. It served her right.

Dexter was puzzled and then ecstatic when he observed Caron park in the church lot, the trooper walk her to the door, and then get in his patrol car to leave. It would be easy to slip into the lot and rake a key down the side of her vehicle. That'd let her know he was still around. He had circled the block a couple of times to check out activity and parked the van on the street against the curb. It was dark enough beyond the reach of the security light to protect his approach to her vehicle. The sound of a door opening made him stop and step back into the shadows of tall cedars.

When Caron stepped into view, he couldn't believe his luck. He could not let the opportunity pass and acted with speed, on her in a flash, a knife at her throat. She had gasped at the surprise.

The sound of children caused him to freeze but a whispered threat in her ear that he would hurt them if she screamed silenced any protest. She had sagged against him in submission. The threat was renewed when he closed the side van door and minimized her struggle with duct tape across her mouth. He tore more tape and started to wrap it around her wrists. This time she kicked, struggled, and he hit her. There was a loud bump when her head hit the metal door and a whimper before she went limp. *That'll keep her quiet.* He calmly started the van, eased onto the street, and drove out of town.

He flipped the high beam lever to provide more light on the highway to search for easy access side roads. There was no need to speed or attract attention. Since he had exchanged the car for a van, his sense of freedom returned and he believed it would be easier to move around without being noticed.

Thoughts of what he wanted to do to her pressed vivid images in his mind. Just the fact she was his prisoner, that he was in control—that he had the power to decide what and when he wanted, created such a physical excitement his butt squirmed in anticipation. *You're mine now.*

* * *

CARON PANICKED. She could feel the nausea rising in her throat. The stink of onions and old grease was so close the odor flooded her nostrils and her stomach rebelled. Tape sealed her mouth tight. Her arms were bound behind and she could not move her legs.

She began to swallow, willing herself to be absolutely still—keep swallowing. If she threw up, she would choke on her own vomit. Inhale. Breathe. Slow. Slow. It seemed forever before the urge to throw up relented. Turning her head away from the smell helped a little.

The bump on the head she received when she was slammed against the van's metal door post was painful. He had slapped her when she began to struggle after the children were out of view. The nightmare she had lived with for so long was now real. Her worst fear pounded a heavy understanding in her chest. She was in real trouble. A muffled protest forced its way through the tape. It was loud enough for her captor to hear.

The van slowed a bit and almost stopped. Caron realized he had pulled off the smooth highway onto a bumpy road. Jeans and a T-shirt were not enough padding to relieve the sharp jolts her body was absorbing from the potholes. When she managed a louder whimper, the van stopped. Caron listened as a door opened.

She willed herself to be very still on hearing the side door latch release. She lay waiting on the floorboard in the dark. Fear oozed from every pore of her skin. Instinct took over but all she could do was bend her knees and pull her legs upward, then scrunch in a fetal position and pray.

The movements she heard were slow, as if each one was controlled and deliberate. That increased the unending emotional horror that streamed through her mind of what may come next. She heard a subtle click and then a flashlight beam paused on her face before it proceeded over her scrunched form. It moved slowly, hesitated on certain parts of her body. Caron cringed. It was as if his hands were touching her private parts instead of the light. All she could do, bound with duct tape, was close her eyes and pray. *Why doesn't he say something?* The snigger of laughter changed her mind about wanting him to speak.

"I gotcha. And there's nothing you can do. Now you're mine."

She struggled but could not get away from the hand on her thigh and its heat pressing into her jeans. A cry of protest rushed into her throat but the tape blocked most of the sound. He stopped when she exerted a strong flinch from his invasion on her body. His hand clamped down hard and remained.

"Bet you didn't object to that state trooper putting his hands on you. You let him. Before I'm through you're gonna love my touch and scream for me not to stop. Now, if you promise not to be trouble, I'll remove the tape. Remember, I got a real sharp knife."

Caron nodded her head and his fingers began to work the corner of the tape. He gave it a quick jerk and she felt the pain all the way to her toes. She wanted to bite the fingers that ran across her lips.

"Such a shame to cover that pretty mouth with tape. Your

ECHOES FROM THE MOUNTAIN

lips are swollen. They'll get better and then I'll make them swell again with my kisses."

Her first thought was to scream in his face, ask why, but she knew better, had to be cautious. He was crazy. *Stay calm, Caron. Just stay calm.*

"Why me? I don't even know you." She willed her voice to remain low.

"I knew right off what you wanted when you bumped into me at the deli. I could tell. That was no accident. You wanted to play a game and have me follow you. But you had to go and get that state trooper involved."

Think, Caron, think. Every muscle in her body went into survival mode. She knew what he wanted, what he was going to do to her, and there was nothing she could do but try to remain calm and not provoke him. There was no alternative but to play along with his fantasy while she figured out what could be done.

"I need to go to the bathroom."

He stared into the dark but said nothing.

"I really need to go to the bathroom¾bad."

"I'll help you outside and you can do your business on the side of the road. That is, if you promise not to do anything stupid. If you do, you'll be sorry."

Think, Caron.

"What's your name?" That got his attention.

"Dexter."

It galled her to say his name, but she needed time to think. When she spoke again, her tone was low and softer. His head jerked to the side and the flashlight beam landed on her face.

"Dexter, please. I can't use the bathroom on the side of the road. I need privacy. Can't we go some place that has a bathroom? That would be so wonderful. It would mean so much to me. Please." The light was so concentrated she blinked. Behind the beam of light his physical outline remained as still as a statue.

She dared to continue to plead her case. "I thought you cared for me. If you do, you'll consider my feelings, too, and my needs as a woman."

The only noises she heard were a sharp whoosh of air and a "humph." He opened the side door and got out. She heard the driver's side door open and felt the sudden jar when he landed in the seat and started the motor. Without the flashlight beam it was pitch dark but she could feel the van move forward, stop, and turn.

Caron had no concept of time. It may have only been a few minutes that lasted forever. She could see flickers of light on the rear window and understood the van was back on the highway. Her mind conjured escape plans and discarded each one as impossible. Her hands and feet were still bound tight. Even if she tried to sit up, he would react. She was wishing she had taken Bill's suggestion about learning how to use a gun. But it would have been in her car and no time to get it before Dexter took her captive. She would have to be patient and watch for an opportunity.

The van slowed and stopped. From her prone position on the floor she could see a Chevron neon sign. She did not move a muscle when the side door opened, he got in quickly, and slammed it behind him. The solid click was unnerving.

"I'm going to untie you. Try to run and you'll get the knife. Understand?"

"I understand. I won't try to get away, Dexter." She made sure when she repeated his name it was soft. His reaction was another, "humph."

He had parked the van at the side of the building, away from any security light. "Come on," he said and pulled her out of the van. After lying in a cramped position for so long, her knees buckled and she almost fell. Dexter reached out to break her fall.

"Give me a minute," she said. "Just give me a second. It's my knees." He released her but stood close.

"We're going inside, and I'll be right behind you. You'd hate to see anyone get hurt if you do anything stupid." He was so close Caron could feel his heat and the nauseous odor of an unclean body. She inhaled the night air to keep from gagging. She assumed with the smell of food in the van and odious reek that wafted over her shoulder that he had been living in the vehicle. He gave her a sharp jab in the back and she stepped inside the convenience store, then another hidden poke for no one to see toward the restroom sign. The young woman at the cash register glanced up at them and then turned her attention back to what she was doing.

A whisper in her ear warned her again not to say a word. "I'll be standing right here," he said and pushed open the door marked women.

When it closed behind her, Caron leaned against the cool wood for support.

She moved to the commode, unzipped her pants, and sat down. *Lord, how do I leave a message?* The tissue she pulled from the dispenser twisted the class ring on her finger. A light bulb clicked in her brain. In a flash, she refastened her jeans and stepped to the wall.

She removed the ring, held it tight, and started to scratch hard on the paint.

Help. 555-1010. *Was that enough? How long will it take for anyone to see this? I need something else.*

The sound of Dexter's subdued voice interrupted her thoughts. "Hurry up. You're taking too long."

Caron started to flush the commode and stopped. She grabbed the plunger and stripped the roll of tissue paper from its holder, tossed it in the commode and rammed it into the hole. Then very quietly she removed the cover on the back of the commode and flushed, pushed the plunger handle over the lever that held the ball cock. The rubber end on the plunger was heavy enough to prevent the commode from reaching the filled level. It would keep running. She hurried to get out of the restroom before the commode started to overflow.

"It took you long enough," Dexter said in a whispered rant when she opened the door enough for her to squeeze through and prevent him from seeing inside. He shoved a finger against her shoulder and she started across the room to the exit door. Her head lifted and she was aware of the attendant's stare. Caron lifted her hand and placed it on the side of her face away from Dexter's vision as if to rub her cheek and mouthed the words, "Help me." She had nothing to lose by trying to get the clerk's attention. That's all she could manage without being detected. He followed too close to do anything further.

On the way back to the van she said, "I'm hungry. Could we not get something to eat?"

"I got stuff in the van, enough for the night. Now, if you're sweet to me, I might stop and get you some breakfast in the morning." His hand landed on the side of her waist.

She reacted without thinking and flinched.

"Oh, so that's the way you want to play. I thought you were being a little too nice."

"I'm ticklish on the waist." That's all she could think of to say.

"Humph. Nothing to eat for you tonight."

He shoved her into the back of the van and stripped more tape from the roll to rebind her hands and feet. Caron lay on the floor and watched an occasional light flicker in the rear window. The smoother movement of the van told her they were on a highway. She prayed someone¾the clerk—would find the message. Dexter didn't drive that far before he pulled off the highway and there was total darkness. When he stopped, she curled into a hunched position and closed her eyes. Then he was in the back of the van next to her. Her gut knotted and she could not get a breath.

He was lying beside her. Her mouth went dry when she felt a hand on her shoulder.

"I've waited months."

She quivered in revulsion when the hand moved down her arm.

"Is that a little shiver of anticipation? You know what's coming, don't you? I bet you're as excited as me." He moved closer and in the pitch darkness she felt his breath on her ear. "I'll wait. I'm going to take you out to that trooper's farm. They'll be looking for you but not out there. I'll leave him with what's left. Don't think he'll want you when I get through."

Caron could not move. Her back was against the seats. If she tried to change positions it would push her closer to him. She would not stop the pools of water filling her eyes. He removed the tape from her mouth, leaned closer, and slid his tongue across her lips, then again to taste her flesh.

"I may not wait 'til we get to the farm."

Caron shut her eyes tight and begged the muscles in her body not to revolt. Chill bumps on her shoulders prickled and spread. *Be calm, Caron. Stay calm.* Going into a screaming fit would be her last alternative. She had not given up on the possibility of talking her way out of danger.

"Go to sleep," he said and turned his back to her.

Caron could not sleep. She remained alert and listened to Dexter's breathing get heavier and finally become ragged snorts.

She was afraid to move¾did not want to risk him waking. The trauma did not ease, but when she was convinced

Dexter was sleeping more deeply, the extreme tenseness began to ebb. The relief didn't last long. It was replaced by panic when Dexter turned over and pushed against her.

"I'll not wait any longer," he said and ripped away the tape that bound her ankles and tried to push her legs apart. Caron began to fight, kick and push her hands against his chest.

"You'll have to kill me first."

Dexter grunted when she hit him hard on the side of his face.

"I'll show you," he said and rolled on top of her.

Caron squirmed and yelled, "Get off me, you freak."

He rammed a hand between her legs and put his mouth in the curve of her throat. She flinched when his hot tongue licked her skin.

Her back was pinned hard against the floorboard because of Dexter's weight. Caron became aware of vibrations and a faint hum. The van began to shake and the sound became a deafening roar. Bright light filled the windows and overrode the dim morning darkness.

Dexter pulled his mouth away from her throat. "What the hell?"

Caron heard the side door slide open and Dexter's weight lift. Heavy swearing and protesting grunts filled the air.

CHAPTER 26

Caron fought the arms that scooped her body from the floorboard.

"It's okay. It's okay, baby. I got you."

The voice she heard released a flood of tears. Bill lifted her from the van and pulled her tight against his chest. Her arms went around his neck to hold on for dear life. She could not tell whether the trembles she felt were from her or Bill.

"Are you okay? Did he hurt you?" His lips pressed against her cheek to ask the questions.

Caron could not speak. The emotional sobs she had hid from Dexter to keep from showing any weakness would not stop. Caron kept her eyes closed but she heard scuffles and Dexter's curses.

She heard an unfamiliar voice. "Let's get her to the back of the rescue truck. We'll check her out."

Caron finally managed to ask, "Have they got him?"

"Wallace is taking care of him." Bill's arms tightened. "I got you. I won't ever let you go."

Caron closed her eyes and allowed the reassurance in his voice to be her blanket of security. She wanted his strong arms to be her forever safety net. He carried her to the waiting rescue truck. The back doors were open and when he started to sit her down she resisted.

"I won't leave you," he said, and sat down beside her.

The paramedic asked if she hurt anywhere as he took her blood pressure and checked her heart rate.

"I'm okay *now*."

"Did he assault you? We'll need to take you to the emergency room so they can check you out."

"No, he didn't rape me. He was trying to."

Bill's hand found and covered hers. He held on tight and she absorbed his surge of strength.

"I'm okay," she said and turned to Bill. "How did you find me?"

"The girl at the convenience store realized you were trying to tell her something and watched when the van left the parking lot. She saw the water seeping from under the bathroom door and made the call when she saw the message."

He pulled a cell phone from his shirt pocket. "I need to call Bruce and let him know you're alright. He's waiting at the police department."

His call was quick and to the point.

"We got her. She's safe. The stalker's in custody. We're coming back to the police department. See you in a while," he said.

"How did you know?" Caron said.

"I was running late and called Bruce to go to the church and wait for you. When he got there, they were already searching for you. The security tapes in the church office showed us what happened¾him forcing you into the van."

"He had a knife and said if I didn't do what he wanted he'd hurt the children."

"It's over. He won't bother you again. He'll be charged

with stalking, kidnapping, and anything else we can hang on him," Bill said.

Wallace walked by with two officers escorting Dexter in handcuffs. Dexter saw her and started yelling. "You played me." He tried to lunge but the officers held him tight.

"Get him out of here," Wallace said. He approached Caron. "You alright?"

"Yes, thanks to you all."

"If the paramedic says she's okay, then she needs to come back to the station. We need to get a statement."

Caron eased from the rescue truck. Bill put his arm around her waist and ushered her to his patrol car. An officer got into the van. It took a few minutes for all the vehicles to get turned around but they filed in a single line convoy back to the highway.

"Come here," Bill said, and Caron scooted across the seat to melt against him. He tried to pull her even closer, slid a hand to the back of her neck and pressed her head against his chest.

"I prayed the clerk would find my message. Those prayers were answered. What happens next?"

"He'll be charged. It will go through the legal system, but when we get through there will be enough to keep him behind bars for a long time. You won't have to worry about this creep."

All Caron wanted was to be near Bill and feel the comfort and strength he offered. She closed her eyes and reveled in his presence, hid the satisfied smile when she felt his breath feather across her face.

She closed her eyes as the miles melted away. Little spurts of light flashed against her eyelids when they reached the city. The patrol car had just stopped when the door on the passenger's side opened. Her head jerked from Bill's shoulder when she heard the voice.

"Caron?"

"She's okay, Bruce."

Bruce took her hand and held firm as she slid across the seat and got out. His arms went around her in a tight embrace.

"Bruce, I'm okay. I'm really okay."

"It was tough waiting when I wanted to be out there and smash this creep's face. Is that him?"

All eyes turned to watch as Wallace and the two officers took Dexter inside.

"He's going into a cell. Thanks for your help, being there when I called." Bill extended his hand to Bruce.

"It was one of the hardest things I've ever done, to stay here and listen to all that was going on."

Bill on one side, Bruce on the other, the three of them walked inside the police station. A young woman Caron had not seen before met them at the counter. "Can I get ya'll something to drink?"

"I sure could use a cup of coffee," Caron said. She didn't expect what happened next.

"I'll go with you," Bruce said. The woman and her friend walked to the back of the office and exited the room.

"We'll wait for Wallace," Bill said. "You'll need to tell him everything."

"I'm thankful it's over," she said.

When Bruce and the young woman returned, Caron did not miss the look of total delight on his face.

He handed Caron a cup of coffee. "This is Abbie," he said. "Abbie holds down the office for the night shift. She kept me from climbing the walls while I was waiting."

Wallace entered through another door. "Caron, let's get you back in the conference room where we'll be more comfortable and I can get your statement." Bill stayed by her side.

"I'll wait for you all out here." Bruce said.

Caron squashed a smile when she turned to see her friend. She realized there was something new about him. He glanced up at Caron and his eyes held the answer. It had a name: Abbie.

Bill's hand sought hers as they walked down the hallway to the conference room. Caron held the cup of coffee in the other hand.

"This is going to take a little while. We could do it tomorrow, but you're okay and I want to get it all down while it's still fresh in your mind. Caron, when Drew comes by tomorrow to get the police report for the paper, he'll also see the arrest report, and, well, you're capable of handling that. I'll be back in a minute. I need a clipboard."

Caron sort of laughed. "I hadn't thought about being a news story." She glanced up at Bill when she sat down and was a bit startled at his lowered head. He was watching, head tilted at an angle as if he'd been studying her, a question in his expression. When she sat down he moved so close his hip pressed against the arm of the chair.

She heard the long, slow breath when he scooted a chair close to hers and sat down. "I thought I'd lost you. I couldn't have handled that."

"I believed you would find me." She stopped talking when she saw the storm in his eyes. It was not a flicker of uncertainty but an eddy of desire that pulled her into its depths.

"I didn't think I would ever love again. I do love you," he said and pulled her from the chair onto his lap.

She cherished the warmth of the arms that gathered her into a protective clasp, and reveled in his declaration of love. "Will you be my wife?"

There was no room left in her eyes for the liquid welling to overflow with the taste of sweetness in his words. The blurry outline of the man beside her confessing love was waiting for an answer. It was clear. She wanted to be a part of his life. "Yes," she said.

The door to the conference room opened and Wallace walked in. He stopped halfway across the room.

"Uh, did I interrupt something?" A wide smile changed his serious expression.

"Yes, you did." Bill returned his friend's smile with his own.

"Then let's get started so ya'll can get back to what you were doing."

"Yes. Let's." Caron started giving her statement from the moment she went back to the parking lot realizing she had left her phone in the car.

He interrupted with questions as she related Dexter had a knife and threatened to hurt the children if she didn't get into the van.

As she got closer to the end of the interview, relief seeped into muscles that had been held for so long in a tense state. Bill remained silent as she related the story but his hand on hers expressed his emotions. She settled in calm reassurance. As parts of the story unfolded, she could feel his body stiffen and his hand clasped hers even tighter. When she began to describe the moments before the door opened and Dexter was pulled off of her, his grip became so tight she winced. He saw the pain in her face and released his hold but it did not hide the agony in his face.

The door to the conference room opened, Abbie entered and Bruce trailed right behind her.

"Thought ya'll would want some coffee. I made fresh." Abbie carried two cups. Bruce balanced a single serving and followed.

"We're finished here. Yeah, we could use coffee. Thanks, Abbie. Caron, all I need is your signature." He slid the clipboard across the table in her direction. She signed without reading a word, ready to put an end to months of fear. All she wanted in her sights when she looked over her shoulder was Bill.

Abbie left with Bruce following right behind her. Caron watched Bill study their exit and he did a half turn to Caron. The quizzical expression he presented changed to understanding and a knowing grin tugged the corners of his mouth.

"We'll head out when you finish your coffee," he said.

Bruce came back into the room and sat down by Caron. "It's been a long night and the end of a terrifying journey for you, Caron."

"You've helped me through so many days and nights. I'll forever be grateful for our friendship and that it led me to North Fork and to Bill." She glanced around at Bill, who stepped close and put an arm around her waist.

"Bill will take good care of you."

Caron pressed her hip against Bill's but directed all of her attention to Bruce. "How about you? When will you be flying home? We want to have dinner before you fly back to Los Angeles. Right, Bill?"

"Let's get you taken care of first," Bill said. "Are you going to be at your friend's place, Bruce?"

"In a while," Bruce said. "You've got my cell number. I'm going to hang around here a bit longer before I go back to Dennis's house." He got up. Caron picked up on the slight tone of urgency in his voice.

"Oh. Something I could help you with?" she asked, in a teasing voice.

Bruce hesitated. "Nah. I got this." A flush of red erupted on his cheeks. "I invited Abbie out for breakfast. She said yes."

Caron interjected, "I said yes, too," Bruce.

Bruce looked at Caron, then Bill. His face lit up with a wide smile of understanding.

"I asked Caron to marry me," Bill said.

"Woo-hoo! Fantastic!" Bruce's arms went around Caron, swept her off her feet and put her back down but not before he held her in a spontaneous hug.

He turned and grabbed Bill's hand. "Congratulations! You got one great girl."

"Looks as if you may be coming back to North Fork at some point," Caron said. "I'm glad you came to North Fork. I'm glad I came to North Fork. I'm glad we're all in North Fork."

He released her, winked, and headed toward the door. "I'll go see if Abbie is ready to leave."

"Call and we'll plan dinner," Bill said.

There was a loud silence when Bruce closed the door. Caron did not attempt to hide the smile. She burst out laughing at Bill's surprised look, and clasped his hand to her lips.

"It appears my friend has been smitten, too," Caron said.

"Yes, he has." Bill's chuckle made Caron laugh even more.

"Are you ready? Ready to go home?"

"Yes. Let's go home," Caron said.

ABOUT THE AUTHOR KAY CAGLE

Perhaps fate intervened when I was eleven- years- old and my first job was delivering newspapers in a West Virginia coal mining community. I was a coal miner's daughter whose parents were from the deep south. It was along that paper route my imagination soared, eyes absorbing seasonal beauty and talking with customers of all skin colors and ages. As a teenager I entered our newspaper contest and wrote a sales narrative on how to acquire new customers. I was a winner and received my first published byline writing about the trip I had won. This was the beginning of a sequence of career opportunities that propelled me into the journalism/ media communications field.

Being trained by a photographer, it led to a photo- journalist position with the local newspaper, then to news reporter. My eyes saw tragic scenes no human should witness. I know there was a guardian angel near on some dangerous stories. I wrote a weekly column and was promoted to feature editor. In 14 years as a journalist, I was honored by the Alabama Press Association for Best Column, Best Feature; responsible for the newspaper winning Best News Reporting, Best Investigative Reporting and Community Service Award. I spearheaded and co-authored "Legendary Locals of Cullman County" an Arcadia historical publication. Opting for a career change, I worked in radio and TV sales, deejayed a prime- time gospel radio show and then photographed and wrote thirty second TV commercials before retiring to write romance novels. I draw on incidents and circumstances that become an emotional base, and my characters...well they could be reflections of people I have met over the years.

Made in the USA
Columbia, SC
07 July 2025